NOV **1 2** 2018

8/2018

To:

RANCHO MIRAGE LIBRARY

D1615780

Retribution

Victor O. Swatsek

Victor O. Swatsek
VOS & Associates
Palm Desert, CA
www.NovelsByVic.com
victorswatsek@aol.com

Library of Congress
© 2018 by Victor O. Swatsek

First published by VOS & Associates

ISBN:_____
ISBN:_____

Printed in the United States

This book is printed on acid-free paper

I dedicate this book to my wife, Elizabeth, who is also my closest friend. She has been my inspiration from the very beginning of my writing career.

I would also like to thank my family and close friends, who have become my first line editors, and have encouraged me to continue this challenging and satisfying journey.

I also want to thank my "muses," Prince Alexander and Prince Blueberry, Cinnamon and now my new "muse," Bentley.

Books published:

Go to www.NovelsByVic.com to read a brief overview about each of my books.

Prologue

Wealth and family sometimes do strange things to people. When is having enough…enough? Being content with having a great wife, possibly several children, having a wonderful job that you thoroughly enjoy, and living comfortably might just be enough for some. However, when *any* of those parts of your life are taken away from you, some people feel that their hearts have been broken and they can't continue living. Retribution, by definition, is, *the dispensing or receiving of reward or punishment, especially in the hereafter.*

Walter was sitting in his library reviewing his business holdings. He stopped what he was doing and sat back in his chair and thought, *I really miss Leonard. It's been one year since Leonard died, and for some reason, I still feel I owe him something.*

They had worked on many deals together over the past twenty-five years, had flown all over the world and had enjoyed their endeavors.

Walter called Duncan. "I need to visit an old friend in Gstaad, Switzerland. How soon can we take off? I'd like to arrive there around noontime."

They landed in Gstaad around noon on a damp and foggy day. They drove directly to the entrance of the *Cimetière de Champagne Cemetery* on Avenue de Champagne. They drove over to the caretaker's office for directions.

The caretaker came outside, saw Walter and asked, "Can I help you?"

Walter walked closer to him and asked him, "Can you direct me to where the Leonard Schultz crypt area is located?"

"Hold on a moment, please," the caretaker, said as he looked up the name in his files. "I can tell you where it *used* to be."

"What do you mean *used to be*?" Walter asked looking puzzled.

"According to our records, everything was picked up and

moved to Chile in South America some time ago," said the caretaker.

"Hello, Rick," Walter said. "Are you aware of another llama ranch in Chile which is trying to sell their wool to the *Balducci Couture*?"

"No, I'm not," said Rick. "But, Mustafa *did* call the other day and asked if we could increase production of wool from our two ranches. I told him that right now we are at peak capacity. The llamas' coats have not grown back enough to be able to shear them. We're also adding more animals, but it still doesn't seem to be enough."

"I wonder if we should buy the other ranch or at least his animals," Walter asked. "Maybe you should go visit the ranch and get a feel for the place."

"I was thinking the same thing actually," Rick said.

Walter had just interviewed Claus Livingston for the position of CFO of his company, Monarch Enterprises. The other applicants just didn't have that certain quality he was looking for. Walter was pleased with the background check that was made and his overall qualifications and hired him. As Walter walked towards the elevator in his building, he suddenly had a feeling that he knew Claus, but he was sure he had never seen or met the man before. His way of talking and mannerisms reminded Walter of someone he used to know. *Maybe that's why I like him*, he thought.

"Mr. Donleavy. We will be installing our mainframe computers as soon as we have the computer room built," said Jason.

"That will be fine," he said. "You are the only other tenant I have in this building."

"I hope in the future that I can give you some support for *your* business one day," Jason said.

"We'll see, down the road," Walter commented. "Have a good day."

Rick went up to the cockpit and said, "Del, let's turn around and go back to Providence. The trip has been canceled."

He came back to where Liz was sitting and held her in his arms.

"Darling, I have some bad news for you," Rick said, as tears were running down his face.

"What is it, Rick? You're scaring me," Liz said alarmed.

Chapter

1

Rancagua, Chile is on the West Coast of South America. The wine journey is one of the region's main attractions. There are vineyards located in the *Aconcagua, Colchagua, Curico, Casablanca, Maule* and *Cachapoal* valleys. These regions yield high-quality grapes and made into wines, recognized all over the world.

An individual had been negotiating to purchase the *Adolpho Vincenti* Vineyards in Rancagua, Chile. The winery had been in the Vincenti family for over a hundred years. Juan Cristobal was actually only the second-generation vintner. The current owner, Juan Cristobal, was getting older and his three sons and two daughters had no interest in managing the winery; therefore, Juan started looking for a buyer. He traveled extensively in Europe and to the United States, to get a feel for how much people liked his wine. He had some marketing done but wasn't satisfied with the results.

Arturo Souza, a wealthy individual had been looking for a business investment for some time. After he reviewed several types of businesses, he decided he wanted to produce wine. He had been a wine connoisseur for many years and had an extensive selection of wines in his personal wine cellar to validate his wealth, but wanted to go one step further. His investment banker and financial advisor in Frankfurt, Germany had had several conversations with Juan Cristobal, the owner about purchasing his winery, complete with a vineyard.

"I have reviewed several vineyards for you," Rolf said. "However, I feel the best one is in Chile. Are you considering moving there as well?"

"Yes, I would. Do you think he'll sell me the winery," Arturo asked excitedly.

"I think he is ready," Rolf said. "However, I must also warn you that two other people have shown interest in his winery." *If I can pull this off, it means a lot of money for me*, he thought.

"Let me take a close look at it," Arturo said. "I would like to meet the owner. I think I can make him a deal that he can live with."

"I will make the arrangements," Rolf said.

Arturo Souza arrived in Chile approximately a year ago, when he finally purchased the *Adolpho Vincenti Vineyards* in Rancagua, Chile. They were already producing world-class wines. He always had a passion for wines and now was his chance to be a bigger part of producing this wine. In his previous life, he was a financial investment analyst for a major company on the East coast. After so many years of making deals, buying and selling companies, he felt that he had had enough, and wanted to enjoy his life. Both his wife and son had passed away, and with no other living relatives, he had decided he needed a major change in his life.

Arturo's closest friend named Rolf Freiburg was also his financial banker and advisor. His office was in Frankfurt, Germany. Over the years, Rolf kept Arturo out of trouble as Arturo sought to change his life.

Arturo purchased a used Gulfstream G550 jet from an executive in England who was retiring and wanted to liquidate most of his assets. They also gave him recommendations for a pilot. After much discussion and reviewing his qualifications, Arturo decided on Gaspar Marceau.

Two days later Arturo flew from London, England, where he had been living for the past year to Rancagua, Chile, on his private jet.

"We might be making many trips to Rancagua if I buy this winery," Arturo said.

"That sounds great!" Gaspar said guardedly. "That means you might be living there for a while?"

"Yes, possibly, "Arturo said. "I also have other business interests in the United States."

Gaspar Marceau had retired from the French Air Force as a fighter pilot, where he had flown many combat missions. After he left military service, he moved around and ended up as a commercial pilot for *Air France*. He didn't like it much because it wasn't exciting enough, so he went looking for a different, more exciting career.

He also had extensive training in hand-to-hand combat and was an excellent sharpshooter. However, his specialty was knives. He could throw them with deadly accuracy. He had a set of twelve, flat knives made to his specifications. He even had all his jackets and coats outfitted with special inside pockets to house his knives. He was suave and liked the women. He preferred short relationships because he was not ready to settle down. He had black hair, neatly trimmed, nearly five-feet-ten, and kept himself in very good shape. His single hobby was to coach and watch professional soccer games. At one time, he had considered playing in a league but found that he liked flying better, and it was more financially rewarding.

Chapter

2

Adolpho Vincenti Vineyards was performing above expectations. Arturo had redesigned the label and was producing a Chardonnay, a Sauvignon Blanc, and a Cabernet Sauvignon. However, six months later and after accomplishing all that, he still felt an emptiness in his life. As he sat on his backyard porch staring into a roaring fire on the outdoor patio, he decided he needed to be busier and wanted a different challenge. He went into the town of Rancagua, to see what kind of city and nightlife they had to offer. He drove his Range Rover into town, parked it and just wandered around to see where he would like to have lunch.

He stopped at the *Mr. Belvedere Restaurant*. He looked at the menu, posted by the front door, and noticed that they had tilapia fish on the menu. He walked inside and saw it was crowded, which was always a good sign. He sat at a table close to the window.

The waiter came over and asked, "What can I get for you, senor?"

"What is the most popular wine that you serve here?" Arturo asked.

"That is easy, senor. It is Cabernet Sauvignon from the Adolpho Vincenti Vineyards."

"Is that right?" A surprised Arturo remarked. "I'll have a bottle of that."

"Very good choice, senor," said the waiter and left.

The waiter brought the wine over to the table, showed him the label and opened it. He poured a small amount into a glass for Arturo to sample.

"Excellent," Arturo said.

"Have you decided yet on your lunch, senor?"

"Yes. I will have the *tilapia* with asparagus and a small amount of garlic mashed potatoes."

"Very good, senor," the waiter said and left.

As he was enjoying his wine and waiting for his lunch, Arturo overheard a conversation at a table next to him.

"I want to sell my ranch," he said. "To make it more inviting, we found a source to sell our wool to a company in Tel Aviv, Israel."

That piqued Arturo's interest. He listened a little longer to get more information.

Arturo finally turned to them and said, "Please excuse me, but I couldn't help but overhear that you have a llama ranch that you are considering selling?"

The man at the other table turned to Arturo, "Yes I do. Why do you ask?"

"I just happen to be in the market for another business investment," Arturo said. "I'd like to talk to you about that it if it's possible?"

"Yes, we can talk about this," he said happily. "Please join us."

"Thank you for the offer," Arturo said. He got up from his table, brought his wine bottle with him and joined the other two people.

"My name is William Devonshire, and my place is the *Santa Rita Ranch* in Maipo Valley."

"My name is Arturo Souza, and I own the *Adolpho Vincenti Vineyards*," he said, as he pointed to the bottle. "I would like to come out to your ranch tomorrow, if possible so that I can see it."

"It's about a two-hour drive from here and in the hills," William replied.

"Just give me the address, and I'll find it," Arturo stated confidently.

"Looking forward to seeing you tomorrow," William said.

"I detect that you're English if I'm not mistaken," Arturo said with pride.

"Yes, I am, actually," William, said. "I purchased this ranch ten years ago, and my wife has been giving me grief over it ever since we came here. That's why I want to sell this place and move back to England, as soon as possible."

"Then I will see you around noon tomorrow at your ranch,"

Arturo said.

They all finished their lunch, shook hands and left the restaurant in the afternoon. Arturo left with an adrenalin rush he hadn't felt in some time. When he got home, he called Rolf Freiberg, his banker in Frankfurt, Germany.

"Hello, Rolf. I may have an opportunity to buy the *Santa Rita Ranch*, which is a llama ranch in Maipo Valley, Chile."

"A llama ranch?" asked Rolf curiously. "What do you want with a llama ranch?"

"It's for personal reasons. I'm going to see the ranch tomorrow. If we can agree on the price, I want to pay cash. The owner wants to sell desperately, or rather his wife does. They want to move back to England as soon as the sale is completed."

"Okay," said Rolf, a little dubious about this venture.

That evening, as Arturo sat in front of his outside fireplace, he rejoiced because another opportunity had shown itself. He started planning for the next page in his life. By the end of the evening, he had figured out another way to destroy a man's life. *Things are working just as I had planned*, he thought.

Chapter

3

Several months later, after Leonard left the company, Walter finally hired a new CFO to manage his financial business interests. After an exhaustive search, and with the help of Frank Richter, Rick's CFO, he hired an individual named Claus Livingston.

"Thank you for this opportunity, Mr. Donleavy," said Claus happily.

"Just take care of my companies, and we'll get along very well," Walter said.

Claus Livingston originally was a page working in the U.S. Congress. He did this while he was going to law school at the University of Maryland. He did well, but the number of hours required to perform various errands for senators was affecting his schoolwork. After six months, he left and got an easier job working in the Pentagon cafeteria. This change allowed him the flexibility to concentrate on his schoolwork and still make some money on the side. He originally got the job because his mother knew several key people working at the UN building. During his second year of law school, he decided that law was not his forte.

While he was working in the cafeteria, he was promoted several times. He ultimately worked himself into a position as the head cashier and was involved with some basic bookkeeping. He found he liked working with numbers and as a result, changed his major to finance. He did well, but it cost him an extra year of schooling. He worked part-time at Monarch Enterprises, in Providence, performing various low level tasks for Leonard Schultz. Since he was part-time, he worked as a contract employee for over a year and had to pay his own taxes and insurance.

Even though his parents paid for most of his schooling, he still had incidental costs to pay. Upon graduation, he quit working for Monarch Enterprise and he went to work for a company in New York. They paid all of his outstanding student loans, so they knew where he'd be at least for the next four years.

As Walter was walking towards the elevator in his building, he suddenly had a feeling that he knew this person, but he also knew he had never seen or met him before. *His way of talking and mannerisms reminds me of someone he used to know*, he thought. *Maybe that's why I like him.* He and Duncan went down in the elevator to the underground parking garage. As they stood there waiting for the doors to open, he kept thinking of Claus, because something was nagging at him.

Walter called Fred. "Fred, I just hired Claus Livingston, as my new CFO. I know you've performed a background check on him and it was fine. I don't know why, but he seems familiar to me in some way, and I don't recall ever having met him. Can you perform a much deeper check on him for me?"

"I'll sure give it a try," Fred said.

"By the way, Fred, how are you and your lovely wife, Danielle, getting along?" Walter asked,

"Just great!" Fred said excitedly. "I may put her to work at my company. It seems that she has some accounting experience."

"That sounds great!" Walter exclaimed, happy for Fred, as he hung up the phone.

The fact that Walter asked him about Danielle suddenly took Fred back to what led up to the time when he proposed to her.

Now I have to do this right, he thought. *I remember walking to the flower shop at the casino, and I purchased eighteen yellow roses, walked over to the elevator and punched the twelfth-floor button. I suddenly became nervous and felt my palms sweating, holding the flowers. We made the slow ascent to the twelfth floor, which seemed to take forever. The doors finally opened, and I stood there frozen until the doors tried to close up. At the last minute, I put my hand up, stopping the doors from closing, and stepped out into the hallway. I walked down the long hallway and stopped when I got to Danielle's room. Now that I'd gotten this far, I was at a loss for words, but I finally knocked on the door. I had to knock several times before the door finally opened.*

"Oh, it's you," she said dully. "I was waiting for room service. What do you want, Fred?"

I still remembered how I clumsily said nothing. Danielle stood there, bathrobe carelessly half closed, revealing that she was wearing nothing but the robe. We stood in the hallway for almost a minute, still saying nothing, and so she just stepped back into her room and slammed the door shut.

After being there in front of her closed door for a few minutes, I started to walk away, not knowing what to say, and thought, "Well, that was painful."

I was two doors down when suddenly her door opened up she stepped into the hallway again, and said to me, "You give up very easily, Fred. Is this the way it's going to be when we're married?"

I quickly turned to her smiling. I was at a loss for words, but finally ran back to her room, wrapped her in my arms and whispered, "No, it's not."

Fred called Walter to reveal what he found out about Claus.

"The reason he sounds so familiar is that he used to work for Leonard Schultz," Fred said. "Probably some of Leonard's teaching mannerisms rubbed off on him. He left your company about three years before Leonard moved to Gstaad."

"That's especially interesting," Walter said. "Because he never indicated that he previously worked for Monarch Enterprises."

"He may not have worked directly for your company because he was a contract labor employee," Fred said. "In other words, he wouldn't have signed the normal paperwork. Many companies work this way. It helps reduce costs."

"Thanks, Fred," Walter said and hung up.

That explains some things, Walter thought, but still doesn't explain why he didn't tell me he worked at my company, even for a little while. It would have been a benefit, which most candidates would have exercised.

Chapter

4

The following morning, while Walter was eating breakfast at his home, he received a panicky phone call from his CFO Claus Livingston at the corporate offices of Monarch Enterprises.

"Mr. Donleavy!" Claus shouted hysterically.

"Calm down, Claus!" Walter demanded. "What's the matter?"

"Our financial database has been hacked!" Claus yelled out. "I cannot access anything! Every department in the building is shut down completely!"

"Settle down for a moment!" Walter said. "Let me call you right back."

Walter called Fred immediately and said, "I'm sorry to get you up so early."

"Not a problem, Walter. What is it?" Fred asked.

"I have a major problem in my building," Walter said assertively. "It appears that someone has hacked into our financial database and has somehow locked everyone out from accessing their computer. Claus, my new CFO, just called me."

"Wow, that is serious," said Fred as he got out of his bed. "As I remember, you had your whole system designed and installed by a top computer hacker who worked for the U.S. Army."

"That's correct," Walter said. "This should *never* have happened."

"Let me see what I can find out," Fred said.

"I would like you to access the financial database using your unique hacker skills and see what you can find out that way."

"Okay, I'll go right over to the office and call you from there." *This breach is very serious*, Fred thought.

Fred hurriedly got dressed and drove over to his office. He sat down and immediately logged onto Walter's database.

After a few minutes, *well, that's interesting*, Fred thought. *I was able to get into the system using some simple hacker logons. However, when I access using the normal way, I cannot get in or even have a screen to look at the database.*

An hour had passed when Fred called Walter and said to him. "It's peculiar that I was able to hack into your system using my simple hacking skills. Yet, as you said earlier, I couldn't get in using the normal sign in and password. That tells me that somebody put a type of *bug* into your system *after* they logged in the normal way."

"Why would they do that?" Walter asked.

"My guess is that they want you to pay them something to unlock the system for you," Fred said. "That would be my first guess."

"Is there any way to determine who or where this originated from?" Walter asked curiously.

"I already looked that up, and the hacker created several hundred firewalls," Fred said. "It will take me a little time to figure out how to take each of those down. In the meantime, don't let anybody access the mainframe. In fact, I suggest you send your entire staff home – even your CFO."

"All right I'll do that," Walter said, fretting that someone was able to do this to his operation, as he slowly hung up the phone. *Now I have to worry that my entire financial empire is visible to anyone who wants to do me harm*, he thought.

Walter called Claus back and relayed this message to him, without telling him what Fred would do.

"Claus. Shut down the operation and send everyone home!" Walter said, sounding agitated. "I will call you when you and everyone else can come back to the office, as soon as we can figure this out."

"Okay, I will do that, Mr. Donleavy," said Claus nervously as he hung up the phone.

As Walter also hung up the phone, he thought, *I'm going over to the office unannounced.*

"Duncan. Bring the car around and hurry. I need to go to my office," Walter said.

"I'll be right there," Duncan said, putting on his coat.

As Duncan drove the car around to the front of the house, Walter was already walking down the steps toward the car.

"Duncan…are you armed?" Walter asked.

"Yes, I am," Duncan, wondering why Walter asked.

They drove out of the driveway and onto highway 23A on the way to Walter's building and his office in downtown Providence.

"Duncan, instead of driving to my normal parking spot on the first level in the underground parking garage," Walter said, "drive through the other two lower parking levels."

He saw that all the cars had left except for one in the far corner of the garage. Duncan finally parked on the same floor level of the underground parking garage.

That's peculiar, Walter thought. *Especially, since I told Claus to send everyone home – including him.*

Chapter

5

"Let's go, Duncan," Walter said as he got out of the car. "Stay alert, in case we run into any unexplained situations."

"I'm ready, Mr. Donleavy," Duncan said as he walked in front of Walter, with gun drawn.

They took the elevator up and walked out into the sprawling white and gray polished marble-walled, lobby. Walter noticed right away that no guard was monitoring the sign-in booth.

"Something is not right here!" Walter said, walking cautiously. "There are always two guards stationed here twenty-four hours a day."

Suddenly a side door opened from a room with a door placard that read MENS RESTROOM.

"Hold it!" Duncan yelled out, as the guard came out drying his hands with a paper towel.

"Whoa there!" said the guard, holding his hands up. "Who are you?"

"I'm Walter Donleavy. I own this building. Why weren't you at your guard post?"

"I just went to the bathroom," the guard said nervously with Duncan holding a gun on him. "There is only one of us here. The other guard went home sick. They're supposed to be sending another guard over, but that was an hour ago."

"Stay here. We may need you later," said Walter, as he walked into the elevator and pushed the button to his floor.

The elevator slowly made its way up to the twelfth floor. As the doors opened, Duncan looked out to see if anybody was still around. He stepped out, with Walter following closely behind him.

Walter looked towards the office where Claus would normally be. He saw him in the distance walking back and forth in the office, talking to someone on the phone. Walter looked at the switchboard phone, which showed all of the extensions, and Claus's light was not on.

"Something peculiar is going on here," Walter said quietly. "Claus must be on his private line. Let's quietly get over there and find out what he's doing and why he is still here."

They cautiously walked over to his office. Claus had his back to them looking OUT through the large window.

"I'll be there soon," Claus said with panic in his voice. "I just have one more thing to do."

Walter walked quickly into his office and said, "What is that *one more thing* that you have to do? I thought I told you to send everyone home – and that included you!"

"Mr. Donleavy, I can explain," Claus said, as he quickly turned around and put the phone down.

"I'm waiting for an explanation!" Walter said firmly. "At the same time, why didn't you tell me that you worked in this office under Leonard Schultz as a contract employee?"

"I can explain that, also," Claus said, now in a panic, with perspiration was running down the side of his face.

"Well….I'm listening!" Walter said getting louder.

Claus saw the gun in Duncan's hand, sat down in his chair, with his face buried in his hands.

"I didn't *want* to do it," Claus said, crying into his hands.

"What *is it you did*?" Walter said, getting impatient. "Come on; I haven't got all day."

"Mr. Donleavy asked you a question!" Duncan walked up behind him, with the gun cocked, and shook Claus by his jacket.

Claus quickly stood up, turned around, ran towards the big picture window, crashed through it, and fell twelve stories to his death.

"Oh my God," yelled Duncan. "He *really* didn't want to tell you, did he?"

"I guess not," said Walter casually looking down. "I suspect he jumped because the alternative, which I think would be prison time or worse. That was more than he could deal with. It could have also been that the person who he was talking to on the phone who may have put him up to this scheme."

"What possessed him to do that?" Duncan asked, still in

shock.

"I'm guessing money," Walter said. "He was obviously weak and was probably talked into it. But in the end, he was more confused about all of this and couldn't deal with it anymore."

Walter called Fred. "Fred, lock down my entire system. I think I found at least the person who created the bug. He also just committed suicide by jumping out of his office window."

"Wow. You *must* be kidding!" Fred said loudly.

"No, I'm afraid I'm not," Walter said hurriedly. "I'll talk to you later after I speak with the police."

"What are you going to do, Mr. Donleavy?" Duncan asked anxiously.

"I'm going to call our Vice President of human resources," Walter said, "and tell him to call all of our employees at home and give them all a week of paid vacation. Then I'm going to call Bryon Worthington, the Chief of Police and have him and his detectives come over here to pick up the body. Next, I'm going to have Fred fly out here to take a hard look at our database and see what has been compromised so far."

I am always amazed at how easily Walter switches gears, Duncan thought.

Walter called his Vice President of human resources and said firmly, "Carl, call everyone and have them stay home for the next few days. We've had a breach of security at the company. I'll call you when to bring them all back. Tell them they will be paid for their time off."

"I'll get right on it," he said, a little concerned. *Good thing we have a disaster relief plan for this type of thing*, he thought.

Walter called the Providence Police Department and said, "My name is Walter Donleavy. I need to speak to Bryon Worthington. It's an emergency."

"One moment please," said the desk sergeant.

"This is Bryon Worthington what can I do for you, Walter?"

"Hi, Bryon. I've got a problem," Walter said. He explained how Claus crashed through a window on the twelfth floor onto the pavement below and killed himself.

"I'll be right there," Bryon said as he grabbed his jacket and left in a hurry.

Soon police cars and ambulance sirens were heard in the

distance.

"Fred, this is Walter. I would like you to fly out right away to my office. I need you to try and figure out how much damage was done, and what it will take to get my company back up and running."

"I'll take the next flight out, Walter," Fred said.

Walter then called the building guard and said, "There will be police coming in the front door any minute. You should see a body on the pavement outside the building."

"Yes, I see it! What happened?" said the guard mystified.

"Don't be concerned for now," Walter said. "I want you to call your guard service and tell them I want ten additional guards here at this building within the next thirty minutes."

"I'll call them right now, sir," said the guard.

Walter then called Ernie. "Hello Ernie, I have a little problem. Are you available to come over to my office building right now?"

Duncan noticed how calm Walter was about what had just happened. *He must have ice in his veins*, he thought.

"Yes, I can," Ernie, said. "Anything special going on?"

"I hired a CFO named Claus Livingston," Walter said. "He just jumped out of the twelfth-floor window and landed on the pavement below, killing himself."

"I'll be right over," Ernie said. *I can already feel this is going to be a special week, he thought.*

"Mr. Donleavy, I think you should sit down," Duncan said trying to comfort him.

"I don't have time, Duncan!" he said. "This is my world, and it has just been torn open for the world to see! I just hope the damage is minimal."

Just then, Bryon Worthington walked in with his detectives and sat down in the conference room to review what happened.

"Thanks, Walter," said the Chief. "We'll take it from here," and walked away.

Chapter

6

It had been a full day since Claus Livingston had jumped to his death at Walter's headquarters building. Fred had worked almost around the clock, trying to tear down the firewalls of the hacker that broke into Walter's financial database.

"How are you doing, Fred?" Walter asked, looking over his shoulder.

"Pretty good, actually," Fred remarked. "I've been able to eliminate quite a few of the firewalls. I'm a little suspicious, though."

"Why is that a problem?" Walter asked curiously.

"It's not so much a problem," Fred replied, "It was easier than I originally thought it should be. That tells me that an amateur did this, and maybe it was only meant to slow you down and create problems for you."

"The next thing I'll have you check," Walter said, "is to see who has accessed any of my files within the last forty-eight hours."

"That was going to be my next task," Fred said.

"Lastly, Claus was on the phone talking to someone as we walked in on him," remarked Walter. "I want to find out for the last forty-eight hours, who had called, who made calls and from which extension."

Bryon Worthington, the Chief of Police had lived in Providence, Rhode Island almost his whole life. Except for a short tour in the Army, he had always worked for the same police department. Bryon started out as a *beat* cop in Providence. Over time, he had done well as a detective and promoted several times. He transferred to Internal Affairs and was successful at getting rid of some *dirty* cops. As he rose through the ranks, the current chief retired, and he was the likely candidate to take his place.

He met Walter at one of the many fundraisers to support the police, and Walter always gave heavily, but anonymously. However, Bryon knew, and as such, they became arm-length friends. He was a little on the heavy side, and you had to wonder how he could get in and out of his squad car. He was about five-foot-ten, with prematurely gray hair, and wore thick glasses.

At the end of the second day, Fred said, "Walter, I tracked down which city and country Claus was talking to before he jumped. It was with Chile and a town called Rancagua."

"Again, Chile. It seems to be coming up in a lot of conversations these days," Walter said, as he rubbed his chin.

"They made the call from a restaurant called *Mr. Belvedere*," Fred said. "Does that ring any bells?"

"No it doesn't," Walter said. "However, the town of Rancagua in Chile does." *There must be a connection of some type that I'm not seeing*, he thought.

Walter said, "It might just be a coincidence, but you know how I get nervous with too many coincidences."

"Yes I do, Walter, Fred said.

Fred knew that Walter has an uncanny ability to recognize when a coincidence presents itself. Some people would look at that and marvel they are doing the right thing. However, in Walter's case, he always proceeds with caution and optimism. Nine out of ten times, he was right to be cautious. The only coincidences Walter liked – are the ones he one hundred percent controlled.

Chapter

7

Fred Tremane was a law school graduate with an MBA degree from the Wharton School of Business in Philadelphia. Well before he graduated, some of the *Big Ten* accounting firms had already courted him.

Years ago, Fred was working for a major litigation law firm, performing forensic analysis. He got himself into trouble when the company set up what amounted to a Ponzi scheme to create nonexistent revenue and hide profits. Unfortunately, the three executives who concocted the scheme had been secretly wire-transferring millions of dollars to a bank in the Cayman Islands, and before Fred knew it, they just didn't show up for work anymore.

Fred was the only one left, and since he reported to the CFO, the Fed's assumed he knew all about it, and he ended up taking the fall. Walter heard about the case and knew some of the principals. He hired the finest lawyer for Fred's defense and, luckily, Fred was acquitted on a technicality. After the trial, Fred wanted to get even, and he knew the only way to hurt them – was in their wallets. Also, he felt he owed the good people that worked at the company who had lost everything.

Fred went after the executives with a passion and within a week, working almost night and day, he had traced the money back to a bank in the Netherlands. He had one of his friends, a whiz computer hacker, tap into and transfer all the money to a bank in Lichtenstein. They no longer had any money to spend or to pay their bills. A note was anonymously sent to the hotel indicating what they had done. With no money, they were flown back to the United States, where the U.S. Marshals were eagerly waiting for them.

In the coming years, Fred worked with Leonard Schultz,

Walter's then lawyer, and COO, performing numerous very detailed forensic analyses for some of the companies that Walter had purchased. Walter saved a lot of money and, in return, Fred was handsomely paid for his research and results. From that point on, Walter found another specialist to add to his arsenal of professionals.

Several years later, Fred opened his own business in Fort Collins and had been doing very well ever since. Along the way, he met a woman who shared his values, and he started a relationship with Danielle Smith. Danielle and Fred had been dating each other for several years. He had almost proposed to her on several occasions, but each time he was embroiled in a massive research project for Walter or one of his newer clients. He finally married her after he almost lost her.

Danielle came into Fred's office one afternoon and announced, "I had just quit my job at the Wagon Wheel Restaurant."

"Why would you do that?" Fred asked curiously.

"I think I can help you with some of your accounting work," Danielle said nonchalantly. "Remember, I was the head cashier at that restaurant for years."

"Maybe we can have you do that," Fred said, smiling at her. "Let me finish up, and we can see how to set you up."

"Thanks, Fred. But I also have an alternative reason for this," she said.

"What's that?" he looked up and asked, now more curious.

"I figure if I'm here with you," she said casually, "I can at least get you to come home at a decent time and have dinner with me."

Fred looked at her, now a little worried. *This might be difficult, he thought. She doesn't realize that I don't have a nine-to-five job.*

Danielle had lived in Colorado almost her whole life. Her parents were farmers and owned a parcel of land in Canon City, Colorado, to support themselves. Don Adams, who was the manager of the Monarch Ranch just outside of Fort Collins, was her older brother. Unlike Don, she lacked the drive and ambition to attend a four-year college. She liked to go out and have fun. Her parents at one time refused to give her any more money, so she decided to move and strike out on her own. She moved from Canon City to Coeur d'Alene, Idaho, to Spokane, Washington, and then to Bend, Oregon. After several years of taking any job just to get by, she became frustrated and went back home.

She finally moved to Fort Collins, and went to the local community college and decided on bookkeeping. She didn't know especially why this subject, but after a few weeks in school, she found that she liked it. While she was going to school, she got herself a job as a host at the Wagon Wheel Steak House in Fort Collins. She stuck it out and received her AA degree in bookkeeping.

"I'm proud of you, Sis," Don said. "Are you going to continue your schooling? If you are, you can stay with Maureen and me while you're going to school."

"Thanks, Don," Danielle said. "I'm not sure what I want to do yet. A few weeks ago, I met this person, Fred Tremane, who was at that barbeque you had. He seems like a nice person. He asked me out on a date for next Saturday. He even said that he might move here and move his business to Fort Collins."

"Well, now take it easy, Sis," Don said quickly. "You're just getting your feet planted on the ground and moving in a good direction. I don't know much about this Fred character, but I'll find out for you if you like."

"No, don't do that just yet," Danielle, said coolly. "Let me feel him out a little, and *I'll* see what he's really like."

Danielle stayed at the Wagon Wheel Steak House for another four years and had dated Fred off and on during this time. Meanwhile, she was promoted to head cashier and now was able to move out of Don's house and get her own place.

Danielle was a blond, five-foot-ten and very attractive. Her light blue eyes were almost a distraction when men looked at her. She came to accept it and didn't let it get in the way of her goals.

Chapter

8

This was a special week for both Rick and Liz. Walter was flying in using the new landing strip they had built at Monarch Ranch. Walter's plane descended onto the never-been-used runway. Everyone was cheering as the plane taxied to a stop next to the hangar.

"Just watching the plane landing, looked great!" Rick said smiling as he helped open the door to the plane.

"Hi, Uncle Walter!" Liz said rushing up to meet him and giving him a big hug. "It's so good to see you. It's been a while since we saw you last."

"Thank you. It's good to be back," Walter said smiling. "If for nothing else, than just the fresh air that you seem to have an abundance of at your disposal. I also have a surprise for both of you."

Just then, Hilda, who was Liz's mother, and Jacob, who was Rick's father, departed the plane.

"Hi, Mother!" Liz screamed with joy. "What a surprise. I'm so happy that you're here!"

"Thank you, Elizabeth," Hilda said, "Since we are here, is there anything I can do to make myself useful?"

"I think there is," Liz said enthusiastically. "You can make us a vanilla Bundt cake with chopped walnuts. Ever since we had a piece of that fabulous cake when we were at Walter's place, I just fell in love with that dessert."

"All right, I can do that," Hilda said with pride. "I will need one of the most important things – and that is a Bundt pan."

"We can go into town, and you can pick out the one you need," Liz said.

"Hi, Dad!" Rick said as he hugged his father. "You need to tell us all about your honeymoon in Hawaii after you get settled in at the house."

"It's good to see you too, son," Jacob said.

Duncan departed the plane last, carrying some of the baggage they all brought with them.

"I have another surprise for you and Liz," Walter said. "Sometime today the manufacturer is going to deliver my new plane right here to your ranch."

"You're kidding!" Rick said with a surprised look on his face. "But my pilot isn't here yet."

"He will also be here today," Walter, said smiling. "Well, that's all of my surprises for the day."

"I think that's plenty," Rick said happily.

"By the way, Rick," Walter sounding serious. "When we get to your house, I need you to write me a check for a dollar."

"Okay. But why?" Rick asked curiously.

"For tax purposes," Walter said beaming. "You have just purchased for Monarch Ranch, my plane over there. Now that it's legal, here is your bill of sale. We've concluded our business so...let's eat."

"Okay, well, that was easy," said Rick.

They all drove over to the main house on the ranch.

On the way over, Walter said, "Rick, I need to apprise you of something that I found out recently."

"What is it?" asked Rick, now sounding alarmed.

"I recently leased space to a company in my building in Providence," Walter said. "I'm afraid that the owner of the company, Jason Segal, may not be who he says he is."

"What do you mean by that?" Rick asked.

"I'm not quite sure," Walter said. "So far, Fred can't seem to find out much about him, other than normal simple things. He's still digging but much deeper and he will let me know as soon as he has something."

"You have a sixth sense about these things," Rick said with confidence. "Is there anything I can do?"

"No, not at this time," Walter said.

Frank Richter also came over to the ranch and greeted everyone. He especially wanted to introduce his new girlfriend.

"Everyone, this is Johanna Mitlander," Frank said proudly.

"Hello everyone," Johanna, a pretty brunette, said. "It's a pleasure to meet you all."

Everyone introduced themselves, as they walked into the house.

"I asked Frank to come over, so we could talk about buying more llamas or alpacas somewhere," Rick said.

"Good idea Rick," Walter said. "Incidentally, how is your new cook?"

"She's great," Rick said. "But, I still miss Diana's cooking."

Frank Richter came from an average Midwestern family and was lucky enough to receive a sports scholarship in lacrosse for the first two years. He was five-foot-six, a little stocky, with red hair, and wore thick, horn-rimmed glasses. His appearance would lead you to believe he was bashful. However, he was anything but timid.

When Frank was about ten years old, he found out he was adopted, but that didn't stop him from loving his adoptive parents. He was naturally unhappy after being told that his biological parents died in a car accident. Because he was still very young, his adopted parents worked quickly and helped him face the sadness. Years later, however, he found out that his biological father, Paul Mathews, was still alive. He was actually a master thief, living and hiding somewhere in Europe. Frank also found out that his father, Paul, had divorced his mother while Frank was still very young. Frank was confused. As such, he went looking for a job, far from St Louis.

Frank didn't have time for a personal relationship at this point in his life and was fortunate to become the new CFO for the Monarch Ranch. This included responsibility for the San Lorenzo Ranch in Carrizozo, New Mexico and the St. Augustine Ranch in San Ignacio, Bolivia. The latter two bred both alpaca and llama for the wool. He also oversaw the White Feather mining operation on the ranch.

He met Johanna purely by accident picking out cantaloupe at the local market. He kept tossing one of them from his left hand to his right-hand several times, when a silky voice said, "You could be a great juggler if you could do that with at least three melons."

Frank turned around to see who said that when he dropped the melon, and it broke into twenty some odd pieces. *I'm in love,* he thought. *She has long dark hair and a wicked smile.*

He smiled and said, "Yeah, I guess that would be great, but I'm trying to figure which of these is perfectly ripe."

"Okay, here's the secret," she said happily, as she told him the very un-complex version of how to tell if they're ripe. "Now you know everything I know about it," and she started to walk away.

"Wait a minute," he said shyly. "I don't know everything…. like what your favorite color is….or what kind of wine you like… or, I don't even know, your phone number."

She turned back to him and said, "My favorite color is blue, I love Chardonnay and champagne, and my number is right here on my business card," as she walked back and handed him her card. "Now you *do* know everything about me…at least the simple things," and she walked away, swaying from left to right, leaving him standing in the produce section with his mouth open and with a broken cantaloupe at his feet.

The next day, he called her, "Hi, Johanna. You may not remember me from yesterday, but I'm the very bad cantaloupe juggler you met."

"Yes, I *do* remember you," she said cheerfully. "Have you learned to juggle three melons yet?"

"Ah….No, not yet," Frank said. "But I would like to take you out to dinner and find out a lot more about you."

Thus began the dating marathon and Frank couldn't wait for the weekend so he could spend more time with her.

Johanna was a brunette, with long hair covering her shoulders. She stands five-feet-five, wearing flats and has piercing hazel colored eyes. She was a lawyer for one of the largest real estate companies in Colorado. She did well but felt she could do more to help the country grow, and wanted to run for a position as city manager of Fort Collins. However, she didn't realize at the time that her whole life was going to be on display for everyone to see. The forms she had to fill out almost took her back to her childhood when she was in the first grade. She wasn't quite sure she wanted to expose herself that much. There were certain parts of her life she did *not* want to disclose. Her divorce from a fellow attorney was brutal and left her in shambles for a while. She also didn't want it to come out that in college she was a little wild, being part of a movement and of course, she had smoked marijuana. However, even though that was all behind her, she still wanted to forget that part of her life.

She went back to being a lawyer for one of the larger litigation firms in Fort Collins. She was up for a partnership, because of her previous accomplishments and wins for her clients.

Chapter

9

Two weeks later, Walter was sitting in his library reviewing his business holdings. He stopped what he was doing and sat back in his chair and thought, *I miss Leonard. It's been one year since Leonard died, and for some reason, I still feel I owe him something.*

They had worked many deals together over the past twenty-five years, had flown all over the world and had enjoyed their conquests.

Walter called Duncan. "I need to visit an old friend in Gstaad, Switzerland. How soon can we go? I'd like to arrive there around noontime."

"I will call you right back, Mr. Donleavy," Duncan said.

Twenty minutes later Duncan called Walter and said, "We can leave tomorrow, with a layover in Lisbon and then on to Gstaad."

"Let's do it," Walter said, now was feeling anxious.

"We can also see how the new plane handles for long distances," Duncan said excitedly.

"Yes, that true," Walter, said and only half listening to the comment as he hung up the phone.

Walter had purchased a new Raytheon 1900 series jet. He had modifications made that included adding an oval-shaped bed, a larger closet, a larger shower and bathroom and an eating area that seated six people. It also had extra-large fuel tanks added for longer flights. He had all of these modification made before he took delivery. The interior had knurled walnut on all wood exposed areas and double stitched, yellow tanned ostrich skin, seat covers, and benches.

Duncan landed at the *Lisbon Cascais-Tejo Regional Airport* in the evening in Lisbon, Portugal, before going on to Gstaad. They had a light dinner at the Lisbon Hotel restaurant. However, Duncan could see Walter was not his normal cheerful self.

Duncan finally asked, "Is there a special reason why we're going to Gstaad?"

"I just want to visit an old friend," Walter said abruptly and let the conversation drop.

In anticipation of the flight to Gstaad, Walter didn't sleep well that night. He finally got up and got dressed while it was still dark outside. He had room service bring him a pot of tea that he drank while he was waiting for Duncan.

Duncan finally knocked on the door and said, "Mr. Donleavy, are you ready to go?"

Walter opened the door promptly and said, "I'm ready, Duncan. Let's go." and he walked quickly past Duncan heading towards the elevator.

Duncan stood there, wondering what was going through Walter's mind.

They took off from Lisbon and finally landed at the *Alpina-Gstaad Airport*. The weather was dreary, similar to the way Walter felt as they landed. After landing and going through customs at the Airport, they rented a car and drove through the streets of Saanon, which was close to Bern and Gstaad.

"Let's drive to the *Cimetière de Champagne Cemetery*," Walter said casually.

Duncan thought he knew who Walter intended to visit, but didn't say anything.

"Oh, I forgot to tell you…it's Leonard," Walter said calmly.

I thought as much, Duncan thought, but didn't want to say anything.

They arrived at the entrance to the *Cimetière de Champagne Cemetery* on Avenue de Champagne. They drove through the large wrought iron gate and over to the caretaker's office for directions.

The caretaker came outside, and said, "Can I help you?"

Walter walked towards him and asked, "Can you direct me to where the Leonard Schultz Crypt area is located?"

"Just a moment, please," the caretaker, said, as he looked up the name in his files. "I can tell where it *used* to be."

"What do you mean *used to be*?" Walter asked looking puzzled.

"According to our records, everything was moved to Chile in South America some time ago," said the caretaker.

"Can you tell me who moved it?" asked Walter.

"I'm sorry, I don't have that information anymore," the caretaker said. "You might be able to get the information from the City Hall in town."

"Thank you. I'll do that," Walter said, wondering why they moved the crypt and drove off.

As they were driving, Walter called Fred. "I need some information. Can you find out from the Alpina-Gstaad, City Hall where they moved the crypt of Leonard Schultz, and his family? He died a year ago and I just found out that his crypt and everything that was in it, was physically moved from the *Cimetière de Champagne Cemetery* to some place in Chile. It was enormous in size and must have cost a fortune to move."

"Okay, Walter, I'll check it out and call you back," said Fred.

Let's go back home, Duncan," Walter said, confused and *still wondering why, and who had moved Leonard's family crypt*?

"It was a man named Horst Heinzinger," said the records clerk. "It cost a small fortune, but he didn't seem to care what it cost."

"Do you have an address in Chile?" Fred asked, now very curious.

"It only says the *Palmyra Cemetery* in Rancagua, Chile," said the Records Clerk.

"Thank you. You've been very helpful," said Fred confused about why someone would spend *that* kind of money to move a family crypt.

Fred called Walter and relayed the information he received from the records clerk.

Walter said still bewildered. "I found that out also. I wonder what's going on in Chile."

"I don't know, but according to the records clerk, it was very expensive," Fred said. "On top of that, once someone is buried, moving the bodies is also a paperwork nightmare."

"Thanks, Fred," and he hung up the phone.

I know I'm not paranoid, Walter thought. *However, if Leonard had no other living family, then who and why did they move the crypt, to of all places – Chile?*

Chapter

10

Walter was secretive about himself and his business, but he did have one business partner – Leonard Schultz. He had functioned as the COO and had prepared for Walter weekly reports on the financial health of his companies. Walter had recruited him directly from Yale.

Leonard was at the top of his class and single at the time. His parents died during the Great Depression, so his grandparents raised him. Leonard's parents were German immigrants from Kaiserslautern, German who came over to the United States in 1925. He had studied international corporate tax and business law. Even though he had several very good offers from prestigious law firms in New York and Chicago, he finally decided to accept the exclusive position from Monarch Enterprises. In the coming years, Leonard became a very wealthy man with only one client – Walter Donleavy.

He stood about six-foot-two, with dark blue piercing eyes, a commanding expression, and a voice to match. He always dressed as if he were going to take over the company they purchased that day.

Leonard had one son named Peter. One of his personal dreams was to have Peter take over the reins of Walter's empire when Leonard retired. Peter, however, had other plans, and they didn't include Walter's business interests – or his father's. He wanted to be recognized as a *player* in the market. Unfortunately, he wasn't quite ready for the big leagues. Consequently, Peter created major problems for Leonard that had an even deeper impact on Walter's business interests and relationships with his clients, friends and business associates.

Because of the problems Peter created, Leonard, feeling genuinely embarrassed, ultimately resigned and retired as COO of Walter's business empire. Leonard moved his family to Gstaad, Switzerland, which he previously used only as his summer home. Shortly after that, Peter had a breakdown. Leonard's wife, Cynthia, fraught with all that had happened, was hospitalized, and several days later, had a heart attack and then died the next day. Sometime later, Peter couldn't face the fact that he had failed, and he took his own life. Leonard never got over Cynthia and Peter's deaths and had always blamed Walter.

Walter and Leonard had heated words, but nothing that Walter said, could convince Leonard it was not his fault. Walter was heartbroken not only that Leonard's son took his own life, but that he lost a true friend.

Walter had decided not to go to the funerals of Cynthia and Peter. He felt he would not be welcomed and could possibly stir things up again with Leonard. He also didn't go to Leonard's funeral, because he couldn't bring himself to go for similar reasons. Over the next several months, Walter lost a lot of sleep over this. Consequently, some of his businesses suffered a little. However, this was what Walter needed as a wake-up call.

Walter owned another company that was managed by Mustafa Shamir, who was the CEO of *Balducci Couture* in Tel Aviv, Israel. The company produces custom-made carpets using the sheared wool from Rick's two llama ranches. He called Walter to review the sales for the last ninety days and the projected sales for the next twelve months.

"Good morning, Mr. Donleavy," Mustafa said cheerfully.

"Good morning, Mustafa. I've been looking at your sales, profit's and your next twelve months' forecast. I must admit you are doing exceptionally well. The chart shows me that your sales have increased by an astounding six percent over the last ninety days. I assume that you're receiving all the wool you need from New Mexico and Bolivia to support your planned growth?"

"That is one of the things I want to talk about with you," Mustafa said. "Both sources are currently sending me all the wool they can. However, it is still not enough. My backlog for shipment of customized carpets is now at around twelve months from the time they order until shipment. I need to reduce that time to under four months, or I will start losing clients."

"What do you suggest?" Walter asked.

"I have been negotiating with another supplier located in Chile," Mustafa said. "It is the *Santa Rita Ranch* in Maipo Valley. An individual named William Devonshire contacted me a several weeks ago and asked if we were interested in purchasing his wool, or possibly even buying his entire ranch. He currently only raises his llamas and sells them to some of the villagers throughout South America, because they still use them as pack animals. However, that business has slowed down for him, and he has over two thousand llamas that he could start shearing and sending us the llama fur."

"That sounds marvelous," Walter said. "What do we know about him and his operation?"

"They started the llama ranch about ten years ago," Mustafa said. "He also asked me to inquire if I knew anybody that might be interested in buying his ranch. At the time, I was very busy with my marketing campaign, so I put it on the back burner. Now I understand that he's sold it to a person named, Arturo Souza. He purchased the ranch from William Devonshire, who is going back to England with his wife."

"That sounds interesting," Walter said. *I like new opportunities, but I am also concerned about coincidences*, he thought. "Well, it sounds like you have things well in hand. I'd say, see if the wool quality is acceptable to you, and then strike a deal.

"I will do that," Mustafa said happily with the conversation.

The Quechua Indian Tribe developed a process and a secret formula in northern Bolivia that had been passed down from generation to generation. The solution is a mixture of the Brazil nut's outer shell, which is crushed to a pulp and squeezed into a solution. The Brazil nut's reproduction depends on the presence of a special orchid, which does not grow on the Brazil nut tree itself. It has a hardwood-like shell, is very thick, and inside it contains eight to twenty-four triangular shaped seeds, which is the actual Brazil nut for eating.

The secret was finally passed on to Philippe Herrera, the man who married Whispering Willow – daughter of Chief Tucatom. Phillip sold the ranch along with the secret formula to Walter to create the silk-like carpets.

Walter called Fred. "Fred, can you do a little research for me? I'm very curious about two names. One is William Devonshire, who owned the llama ranch, who is also moving back to England. The other is Arturo Souza. Both are from Chile, who actually bought the ranch."

"I'll do that and let you know shortly," Fred said.

The country, Chile, it seems, is coming up in many conversations these days, Walter thought.

"Hello Rick," Walter said. "Are you aware of another llama ranch in Chile that is trying to sell their wool to the *Balducci Couture*?"

"No, I didn't know that," Rick said. "But, Mustafa called me the other day and asked me if we could increase production of wool from our two ranches. I told him that right now we are at peak capacity. The llama's coats have not grown back enough to be able to shear them. We are also adding more animals, but it still doesn't seem to be enough."

"I wonder if we should buy the other ranch or at least his animals," Walter asked. "Maybe you should go visit the ranch and get a feel for the place."

"I was just thinking the same thing," Rick said. "Mustafa said that his carpets are selling very well and that he's starting to penetrate the European market."

"Yes. Mustafa started a campaign about a year ago, and it is finally coming to fruition," Walter said.

"All right then. I'll schedule a trip over there in the next day or so," Rick said. "I'm going to probably take Frank with me to also get his take on the new ranch."

"Good idea," Walter said and hung up the phone.

Chapter

11

Walter had Richard Teaubel's name changed to Rick Benedict after he came over from West Germany in 1955. He was only five years old and stayed with his uncle, Walter Donleavy, while he was going to school. Since Rick didn't speak a word of English, Walter hired a special tutor to teach him the language. Four months later, still with a slight accent, he was enrolled at Mount St. Albans, a prominent military prep school in Providence, Rhode Island.

When he graduated, he went on to St. Basil's, which was also a private school in Providence. He received his Bachelor's in history and completed his Master's in art and architectural history from Columbia University, majoring in the historical European era. He received his second Master's in mechanical engineering, also from Columbia. At the time, he was considering being a high-rise building engineer. Rick knew he liked teaching and several excellent universities had courted him.

After a year of teaching, Rick got his notice in the mail from *Uncle Sam*. It said he was drafted into the Army. Since he had degrees in several subjects, they recommended that he apply to Officer Candidate School (OCS). After a battery of tests during OCS training at Fort Bliss, Texas, the Army felt he had a higher calling and gave him orders for Advanced Infantry Training (AIT) at Fort Belvoir in West Virginia. After completing the training, he was promoted to Second Lieutenant. His first assignment was as a Nike Hercules Missile Repair site and was stationed in Zweibrucken, Germany.

However, after two years, that quickly grew boring because it wasn't challenging enough. Rick wanted to do something more exciting and fulfilling. As he finished his tour of duty, he was repeatedly asked to re-enlist, but each time he declined.

"I want to get back to teaching, sir," Rick said to the Major Recruiting Officer.

Rick was handsome, with a chiseled jaw, blond hair, and blue eyes. He left the service, went back to school and became a professor at Brown University. Over a period of four to five years, he'd taken a break from teaching and helped Walter with some of his problems related to some new businesses he purchased. It also became financially rewarding for Walter as well as for Rick.

Using the skills he learned in school and the service, he turned a ranch that was used to entertain clients, into a working cattle ranch. They renamed it – Monarch Ranch. He also continued to manage two llama and alpaca ranches. One was the *San Lorenzo Ranch* in Carrizozo, New Mexico, and the other one was the *St. Augustine Ranch* in San Ignacio, Bolivia. Both had proven to be a worthwhile investment to support *Balducci Couture*, the manufacturer of high-quality carpets.

Mustafa Shamir was the CEO of *Balducci Couture* in Tel Aviv, Israel. Before that, he was in the illegal arms business, supplying weapons of all sorts to anybody who could pay his price. He worked out of a warehouse on the outskirts of Tel Aviv, Israel. While his arms business was very profitable, it was also more dangerous. He sold his arms business to his cousin in order to becoming a full-time rug merchant, which was became his first love.

Because of his previous experience in creating and selling rugs, Walter made him an offer to become the CEO of *Balducci Couture* located in Tel Aviv. He was now a major player in manufacturing high-quality silk-like carpets from the wool of the llama and alpacas. Over the years, his business prospered. The carpets became very popular due to their softness, color, and durability. They developed new outlets all over Northern Africa and the United States to compete with the large carpet manufacturers who sold theirs around the world.

Chapter

12

"Honey, how would you like to go to Rancagua, Chile, with me?" Rick asked.

"That sounds like fun," Liz said, as she curled up in his arms on the sofa. "What are we going to do over there?"

"There is a rancher with about two thousand llamas, who has contacted Mustafa about buying his raw wool," Rick said. "While I know this guy had just bought the ranch, it would be a good way to accelerate building up our herd at our St. Augustine Ranch in San Ignacio, Bolivia. He might just want to sell his ranch in Maipo Valley, Chile. It all started because Mustafa's business is growing so well that he can't keep up with the demand, plus he's falling behind in delivering them to his clients. We want to make sure his business keeps growing, which means we need to find other llama and alpaca ranches."

"We can take our new plane, can't we?" Liz asked excitedly.

"Yes, we can. In fact, I'll call Del right now and ask him when we can take off," Rick said enthusiastically.

"Del, this is Rick. We want to plan a trip to Rancagua, Chile. How soon can we take off?"

"I just want to make some final checks, and we can probably take off tomorrow morning if you want."

"Great. We'll be ready," Rick said, and he hung up the phone.

Del Babinski was the pilot Rick hired for the Monarch Ranch. Duncan Houston interviewed him along with three other pilots, who all had a commercial pilot's license. The fact that Del had over one hundred thousand miles under his belt is not a big thing in itself. However, they were also some of those air miles flown in Vietnam, dodging bullets, which was one of the key considerations. He had flown Hughes Helicopters primarily when he was in Vietnam.

He was about six feet tall, with a short crew cut. He played football both in high school and in college. After playing college football for a while, he started worrying about the possible injuries you could get, which could put him out of commission. He felt there were no big job openings for helicopter pilots with leg or head injuries. He was licensed to carry a firearm, and his weapon of choice was a SIG SAUER P226 TACOPS, Semi-automatic, 9mm, 20 round capacity. He always carried a pair with him.

He was not married but kept in touch by long distance with a woman he'd been seeing when he was living in Provo, Utah. It was an off and on type of relationship, which was mostly off because he was flying so much.

Now that I've moved permanently to Fort Collins, he thought, *there might be a chance for a more permanent relationship, but only if I can get her to move out here with me.*

He called her and cheerfully said, "Hi Gail. I haven't talked to you since I moved to Fort Collins."

"Hi, Del. It's good to hear from you," she said cheerfully.

"What are the chances of you flying out here to visit me in Fort Collins?" Del asked.

"I guess I could," Gail said, apprehensively. "When would you like me to come out?"

"I've got to fly out on an assignment in the morning," Del said. "I should be back in about three to four days. How about if I call you when I'm on my way back?"

"Okay, but I'll have to let my boss know at least a day ahead of time," Gail said.

"Great!" Del exclaimed. "I'll set it up with a ticket waiting for you at the counter," he said and hung up, a little happier than before he called her.

Chapter

13

The next day around noon, Rick, along with Liz and Frank took off for Rancagua, Chile. Rick decided that he wanted to sit in the copilot's seat so he could watch as they taxied on the runway and then flew off.

"That was exhilarating, Del," Rick said. "I haven't been in the cockpit in a long time."

"What are we going to do in Rancagua?" asked Del.

Rick explained that he had two llama ranches that supplied their wool to a company called the *Balducci Couture* located in Tel Aviv, Israel.

"It seems that all the wool we produce still isn't enough to keep up with the demand," Rick said. "They make these fantastic custom-made carpets. They are in high demand and backlogged around twelve months."

"No kidding," remarked Del. "These must be some special rugs they make."

"You have no idea," Rick said rolling his eyes. "Next time you're up at the main house, take your boots off and walk on the carpet that we have in the living room. They're not only fantastic to feel, but the rich colors are beautiful as well."

"I'll have to try it when we get back," Del said.

"This new ranch we're going to see could be a real find," Rick said to Frank. "When we get back, we should sit down with Mustafa and see what his actual projections are. This new place may not even be enough if he's growing as Walter indicated."

"I'll get Mustafa's projected sales and see what he needs not just for today, but for the next five years," Frank said. "This should be interesting having three llama ranches and possibly more. You know, based on Mustafa's projected sales and the number of carpets he's planning, we might want to establish a breeding ranch."

"That's an interesting thought," Rick said.

Walter had changed Elizabeth Bowen's, name to Elizabeth Hildebrand, and came to Providence, Rhode Island, in 1956 when she was five years old. She was an immigrant from Linz, Austria when her parents shipped her to the United States to live with her Uncle Walter and to get an education. She enrolled in Sister of Passionate Sorrow, an exclusive school for girls in upper New York. She studied the English language from a very early age.

She graduated with honors and had offers from top Ivy League universities. She settled on Radcliffe University because they had the best classes for her long-term goals. She graduated from Radcliffe, with a Bachelor's degree in political science. Liz went on to Columbia University for her Master's and Ph.D. in languages. By the time she graduated, she was proficient in six foreign languages. She had an offer to work at the U.N. as a multiple language translator, but declined.

Over the next few years, she gained certain academic notoriety, which brought her continuous requests to lecture at other universities in the United States as well as in Europe. She recognized the need for a more challenging role, which also turned out to be financially rewarding for her. Liz took her job seriously, but she also wanted to have fun. She ultimately moved onto her yacht full time and enjoyed the different countries she would sail to and give lectures.

It was while Liz was in Europe lecturing that she took up painting. She started creating postcard size oils on canvases and sent some of these to her Uncle Walter. When he received them, he was so elated that he had them framed and hung them proudly in his study. All of her paintings were just signed "Liz" and year date.

She found out just recently that Hilda, who was Walter's housekeeper, was actually her birth mother. Initially, she was extremely angry because she had was told that her mother and father had died in the war. For twenty years, while she was going to school, she never knew that Hilda was her mother. After a long conversion with her, Liz understood the reason for the deception, but it didn't make it any easier to accept. Her father Christopher had died shortly after they immigrated to the United States.

The lecturing circuit was great, but Liz also wanted to do something different besides teaching and lecturing. She talked Rick and Walter into letting her take on the Three Forks Restaurant and Lodge project that Walter had just purchased. With the help of Jacques Béarnaise, Walter's general manager of *The Alpinhoff Restaurant* in Providence, and *The Matterhorn* in Manhattan, they began to transform the chain of twelve properties into a resort style lodge. Within two months, she reorganized the executive staff, reworked the menu and created a new marketing plan to entice a more diversified crowd to stay and eat there.

Even though it was hard work, she had fun with the Three Forks Restaurant and Lodge project. All the locations were doing very well. She reorganized the restaurants one more time and was able to structure the organization so that she only had three general managers reporting to her. They built the enlarged barn-like building on four of the restaurant properties and started being a draw not just for some locals, but also it became a retreat for some larger businesses from other states.

Chapter

14

The same day that Rick was flying to Rancagua, Chile, Walter had lunch at his latest restaurant, *The Blue Lobster*, located in Mystic, Maine.

As Walter walked inside, he was met by Milton, his General Manager.

"Good day, Mr. Donleavy and Mr. Houston," Milton said being friendly.

"Hello Milton," Walter said. "It looks like a full house tonight, and it's only Wednesday."

"Yes, it is packed," Milton, said smiling, as he looked at the crowd.

As Walter looked around, he saw an individual that he hadn't expected to see – Claus Livingston having lunch. *Now I am curious,* Walter thought, hoping he wouldn't see him. *Just a coincidence I suppose,* he thought. *However, this is a long, out-of-the-way place to go for lunch.*

"Come this way, please," Milton said and took him to a table that was always available for Walter.

"Milton. That gentleman over there," Walter said pointing across the room to the far corner. "Does he come here often?"

"Yes he does," Milton said, looking in that direction. "Normally he is here with another man. They come here about once or twice a month. Today, however, he is alone. I think he's waiting for someone."

"Thanks Milton," Walter said. *I wonder if that man is* – Claus Livingston, he thought.

"Duncan, have you ever had calamari?" Walter asked, still thinking about seeing Claus.

"No, I have not. But it sounds horrible," Duncan said as he crinkled his nose.

"It really is quite good," Walter said. "This calamari are octopus steaks. They cut these about a half-inch thick, marinate them in milk, and a spice solution, and let it sit overnight in the refrigerator. They never seem to have enough. It's a big hit with the angel hair pasta in white garlic flavored cream sauce.

"No thanks. I'll stick to my fried shrimp," Duncan said.

"You don't know what you're missing," Walter said, holding a piece up to him.

Milton de La Cross had been a chef working at Walter's Alpinhoff restaurant for over fifteen years. Jacques Béarnaise trained him, who was the previous general manager. He started out in New Orleans working on a shrimp boat. Everyone that worked on the pier knew how to cook crab, lobster, shrimp, and especially langostino with angel hair pasta. He loved the people, who always seemed so happy, and the food was simple to make but delicious.

He started working at the *Crab and Lobster Brasserie* in New Orleans. Within a short time, he was creating new dishes using those main ingredients. After spending a year there, he left and traveled, working at various places until he got to Memphis, Tennessee. He was lucky to be tapped to be the personal chef for one of the major country western entertainers.

Milton looked like he could take care of himself, but avoided violence. He was tall, slim, with a neatly trimmed dark beard that seemed to wrap itself around his ear and encircle his mouth. He figured he needed a look that commanded attention. Jacques Béarnaise, who was in Memphis attending a wedding at the same time, saw Milton and watched how he cooked his dishes. Jacques made him an offer, which he readily accepted.

"I remember watching you cook when I was in Memphis and was very impressed with the quickness of the dishes you prepared for the tourists," said Jacques. "I want you to keep that same flair, but here we would like to kick it up a few notches. Remember people come here not only to eat, but also for the ambiance, and where they can feel comfortable without wondering if the person at the next table is going to bother them because they may or may not be a celebrity.

"I understand," said Milton. "I hope to one day also have a place like this."

"You will, one day, have that opportunity," said Jacques. "The key is to recognize when that opportunity comes your way…. and grab it."

Over the years, Milton helped create many signature new dishes to complement the current menu. Jacques took notice of Milton and his ability almost immediately. Once he was on board at *The Alpinhoff*, Milton seemed to shine, because he now had the opportunity to create dishes that catered to a different level of clientele.

After dinner, Duncan drove Walter back to his home.

It was a long drive just to have lunch, but I feel it was worth it, Walter thought. "We need to do this more often Duncan."

Works for me, Duncan thought.

They drove up Highway 95. Walter always enjoyed the ride in this part of the country and this time of the year. There was a slight chill in the air, and the leaves on the trees were starting to turn every color you could imagine. Soon they would go through the ritual of falling off and blanketing the highway and streets to create a brilliant, multi-colored carpet. Even though it was dark, with the moon trying to shine through the thick trees and the streetlights, it was still a splendid sight.

They finally arrived at Walter's home and drove through the magnificent wrought iron gates that always seemed to open effortlessly. They took that long winding drive, over the white rock crunching under the weight of the car, to the front of his home.

"Thanks, Duncan," Walter said. He closed the door of his car and watched Duncan drive off to park the car in the garage.

As Walter walked up the four steps to the front door, he

noticed a large case that looked like a wooden wine case. *Hello, what's this*, he wondered. There was a card attached to the box that simply said,

"Please enjoy."

He called out to Jacob, who happened to be walking by, and said, "Where did this come from?"

"I don't know, Mr. Donleavy," Jacob said perplexed. "I didn't bring it. However, the bigger question I have is – how were they able to get through the security gate unnoticed?"

"That is strange," Walter said, puzzled since he had such high security surrounding his entire estate. "Can you take it somewhere else? I'm concerned it may be poison. In any event, I'm sure not going to open or drink it.

Jacob said, "I'll take care of it," Jacob looked at it carefully and felt comfortable picking it up. As he did, he heard a "click," and the case immediately exploded, throwing Jacob off the front steps and about hundred feet into the garden. Walter heard a loud explosion and feared the worst. He ran back outside and tried looking through the smoke that was still in the air.

"Jacob….Jacob…Where are you?" Walter yelled out.

As the smoke started to clear up, Walter walked down the steps. That's when he saw Jacob crumpled up in the flowerbed. His shirt and jacket were torn to shreds, to reveal his chest, hands, and his face that was all bloody. About that same time, Duncan came running around the corner, guns drawn, trying to see through the thick smoke.

"Mr. Donleavy, where are you?" Duncan yelled out.

"I'm over here, Duncan," Walter said aloud, kneeling over the body of Jacob.

Walter tried to feel for a pulse – but there was none. *The assailant had done his job well*, he thought. *The only thing was – they got the wrong person.*

"Duncan call the police and hurry," Walter said choking up.

Walter was in tears as he knelt down next to his trusted, friend who he had known for over forty years. Soon police sirens were heard in the distance, and Duncan opened the electronic gate to let them inside the compound. The police cars entered the compound grounds, and four police officers and two detectives got out of their cars and came over to where Walter was still kneeling.

"Mr. Donleavy, you'll have to step back so we can see what happened," said the Detective. "I see broken wine bottles everywhere. Can you tell us what happened?"

Walter slowly stood up, visibly shaken, and slowly said, "There was a case that appeared to be a wine that showed up on my doorstep while I was out," Walter said. "It was obviously booby-trapped with some type of explosive. I was concerned and asked Jacob to take it away. No sooner was I in the house, when this explosion occurred. The next thing I knew, as I came outside, I was in this thick smoky cloud. Then I had Duncan, my head of security, call you."

The ambulance came and carefully picked up Jacob and put him on a gurney and loaded him into the ambulance. Soon Hilda drove up in her golf cart to see what the commotion was. She saw Walter standing close to the flowerbed, with his bowed down as the paramedics took a draped body and put it in the ambulance.

"Oh *no*, it can't be!" Hilda cried out.

Walter heard Hilda, turned to her, and went to comfort her.

"I'm so sorry Hilda," Walter said, with tears running down his cheeks. "I'm going to find the person who is responsible. I will use all my resources available to find out who did this."

"Mr. Donleavy," said the detective, "I overheard what you said. I think you should let us find out who did this."

"Yeah, that's fine," said Walter, sounding annoyed, and walked Hilda up the steps to the house.

"Mr. Donleavy," Duncan said, "is there anything I can do right now for you? I feel like I have failed at my job to protect you."

"Not at the moment," Walter said. "And yes... you did fail at protecting me, but we'll talk about that later."

He continued walking into the house with Hilda and closed the door behind him. They walked into the living room, and Walter sat Hilda down in one of the large Queen Anne chairs, tearing up as she sat down.

"I'll be right back," Walter said, as he walked over to his liquor cabinet, pulled out two of his special cut crystal brandy snifters, and poured each a small drink. "Here, drink this, Hilda. It may help a little."

Now I have to call Rick and tell him that his father is dead, he thought. *Why somebody would do this is maddening,* he told himself.

"I have another call to make… be right back," Walter said and called Ernie.

"Ernie, I need you to come over to my house immediately," Walter said. "Jacob was caught in an explosion and… now he's dead."

"Oh my God!" Ernie said. "I'm on my way. Try not to let the police take everything with them so I can see some of the debris. See you soon."

Chapter

15

How do I tell Rick that his father has just been killed? He wondered. Especially since Rick only found out that Jacob was his father about five years ago. There doesn't seem to be an easy way to do this.

Walter knew Rick was flying on his way to Rancagua, Chile to look at a llama ranch.

"Rick, its Walter. I have some bad news about Jacob... your father....he is dead."

"What? When did this happen?" Rick asked, devastated. "But I just talked to him yesterday!"

Walter relayed to Rick what had happened.

"Here is what I think we should do," Walter said. "I know you're on your way to Chile. I want you to cancel that trip and come home to my house in Providence. I know that Liz is with you, so please tell her for me. I'll call Mustafa and tell him not to accept any wool from that new ranch in Chile. He'll just have to make do with what he has for the time being. We'll talk about this a little more when you get here. Fred is already here, but for a different reason. Right now there are far too many coincidences and that always makes me nervous."

"All right....we'll turn around, and we'll see you when we land," Rick said somberly. *I never even got to say goodbye*, he thought, as he slowly put the phone down.

He looked at Liz, and she knew something was wrong.

Walter called for Duncan, and said, "Come inside right now!"

Duncan rushed in and stood in the hallway facing Walter's library entrance, brandishing his two Glock guns.

"Duncan, until I tell you otherwise," Walter said angrily, "I will want you to check *every* vehicle, including the golf carts, for explosives of any type. I want this accomplished *every* day at different times of the day. We are not going out for a while. However, you'll have to go and pick up Rick and Liz from the airport when they arrive."

"All right, Mr. Donleavy," Duncan said, looking unhappy and frustrated.

"Mustafa, this is Walter Donleavy."

"Yes, Mr. Donleavy," he said, sensing a problem.

"There have been some unusual circumstances that have happened recently," Walter said. "For the time being, do not negotiate with that new company in Chile. You'll have to make do with what you have for now."

"Yes, Mr. Donleavy," said Mustafa. "Is there a problem I need to be aware of?"

"I'll fill you in later," Walter said. "However, just be careful of anything out of the ordinary happening," and he hung up.

Duncan Houston was born in Calimesa, California. He was an average student in high school, with no particular calling. He decided to join the Marines after graduation. He did his boot camp training at Camp Pendleton in Oceanside, California. He found he had a knack for firearms and felt that this was his true calling. He also worked out and was at one time a participant in the Mr. Universe contest.

Duncan graduated from boot camp and was anxious to know where his first assignment would take him. One morning after roll call, his platoon sergeant asked to see him in his office.

"Private Houston," barked his sergeant, "how would you like to go to Maryland for specialist firearm training?"

"I'd like that very much, sir," said Duncan, grinning from ear to ear.

"Don't call me, *sir*!" said the sergeant. "I work for a living!"

"When do I leave?" he asked, hoping he hadn't screwed up his big chance.

"Go pack your gear, son. You're leaving tomorrow morning at 0600," barked his sergeant. "Don't make me regret this. Now get outta here!"

The next day Duncan was on a plane out of San Diego, to Aberdeen, Maryland. He spent six months gaining a thorough understanding of all the weapons that soldiers used. He then volunteered for a tour in Vietnam. After serving two tours of duty, he became one of the instructors in Vilsec, Germany, who taught NATO officers all about the various weapons in the U.S. arsenal. That was where he met Stephen Weisen.

Duncan was also asked to train as a Seal for the U.S. Navy and was involved in several high-level black-ops missions that still considered classified. After his last assignment on Grenada, the missions didn't seem to provide the same rush of adrenalin anymore. It seemed like just another job. He took that as a sign and decided to retire from the service. After twelve years, he left with the rank of sergeant first class. He stood sixfoottwo, was very muscular, sported a simple gray mustache, and had short-cropped prematurely gray hair.

While he was still in the service, Duncan had developed a relationship with a girl he met one night while they were at the local *watering hole*. He saw her from across the room and just knew he had to meet her.

He walked over and introduced himself. "Hi. My name is Duncan."

"You've been looking at me for almost an hour," she said smiling. "My name is Cynthia. I almost walked over and introduced myself to you because you were staring so long."

They hit it off almost immediately. They went out several times and things were moving along nicely. After their last date, she broke the news to him.

"I'm sorry Duncan to have to tell you this," said Cynthia, "but my ship is deploying in two days, and I don't know when I'll be back."

"I didn't know you were in the service," said a bewildered Duncan.

"I didn't mention it because I never thought we were going to get this serious," she said sadly. "But after a while, I started to fall in love with you, and I didn't know what else to do."

"You could have told me, for openers!" said Duncan, sounding disappointed.

He stood up from the table, walked out to the parking lot, and left without looking back. That was the last time he saw or heard from her. As he drove away, he felt a huge loss.

Duncan found out later that she was married to a Commander in the Navy and that *he* was actually deployed. She merely went back home.

Chapter

16

Jacob Teaubel and his first wife, Geraldine, came over to the United States as immigrants on a United States Liberty Ship called the General Balou. Walter helped them to immigrate to the United States after the war. Jacob knew Walter when they were working at Sachsenhausen Concentration Camp. His wife had passed away while working on Walter's estate several years later, and Jacob had no desire to socialize because of the love he had for her.

He was the gatekeeper and chief gardener for Walter's home in Providence. He had a little house close to the gates and monitored everyone that came to see Walter for any reason. Finally, after many years, they finally installed an electronic gate system, so he wouldn't have to perform that task anymore.

His son was actually – Rick Benedict. He, along with Hilda, also wanted to keep it a secret from Rick that he was his actual father. All the while, Walter told Rick that his parents had also died in the war. It was even a bigger shock to Rick when he realized that Jacob was his birth father.

"All those years when I would visit Walter," Rick said tearfully, "it was *you* letting me in at the gate."

"Yes, it was, and I am sorry to have deceived you," Jacob said sadly. "But at the time it seemed like the right thing to do. We wanted to make sure you had no obstructions going to school and succeeding in the world."

Hilda Lowenstein was Walter's housekeeper and cook

on his estate. Hilda was also incarcerated at Sachsenhausen Concentration Camp during the war. She had worked as a cook and tailor for Colonel Matthias Theisson when he was stationed at the camp while he was a Nazi in the SS.

After they were released, Walter kept in touch with Hilda and promised to help with her child's education when he could. Her daughter was actually – Liz Hildebrand. Hilda wanted to keep it a secret from Liz that she was her actual mother. All the while, Walter told Liz, at the request of her mother that her parents had died in the war. It was a shock to Liz when she realized that Hilda was her mother. Anna Bowens was Liz's real name, and she changed it when they came to the United States.

In return, Walter had a house built for Hilda and Christopher, her first husband, toward the back of his estate, and had the freedom to come and go as they pleased. Hilda and Christopher were very lucky to have found each other after the Russians liberated the camp. Since they lived in the same town, they both left together.

Hilda and Jacob's spouses passed away almost twenty-five years ago. They spent some of their days consoling each other, grateful that they lived through the cruelties of war. Hilda and Jacob finally married and divided their time between Providence and in Fort Collins at the Monarch Ranch.

Chapter

17

"Steve, this is Walter. I need some extra security here at the house."

"Okay. Is everything all right?" Steve asked.

"No. Everything is *not* all right," Walter said. "Jacob…has been killed..….right here at my home. I think it was actually meant for me."

"Holy smokes! I'll be there as quick as I can," Steve said. He made a few quick calls to have five of his security people meet him at Walter's house. He hurriedly chartered a jet and brought another five people with him.

When Steve was in the air, he called Walter, "Five people are going directly to your house, and they'll wait for me in the front of your gate."

"Thank you, Steve," Walter said, still feeling the pain of having lost his best friend.

Steve Weisen graduated from Annapolis in 1973, served several tours of duty in Vietnam and Korea. He finished out his service in Germany. When he finished his tour, Walter was waiting for him with a special job. He wanted him to be a ship's captain, but not just any ship's captain. Steve was an expert in hand-to-hand combat and knew how to use almost any weapon. Walter paid him well, even though Steve owed Walter since he also helped Steve's parents flee from Austria.

His parents also lived on Walter's estate. Up to now, Steve had no real personal life, until he recently met Dorothy in San Francisco. His father, Aaron, helped Walter from time to time when Walter needed some cabinet work done. He helped outfit the boat Walter gave to Liz, which was named *Federico.*

Steve was tall, with blond hair, steel blue eyes, and a rugged look. He did have one hobby, and that was scrimshaw carving.

It was around 1972 when Steve left the service and came home to see his parents. One day Steve got a call from Walter who said, "Steve, can you meet me tomorrow morning at the Conanicut Harbor?"

"Yes, I can," said Steve, wondered what Walter had in store for him. "I'll see you there."

The next morning Steve drove out to meet Walter at the harbor.

They were casually walking on the pier towards the boat slip when Walter said, "The job is as the ship's captain for my niece. Her name is Elizabeth Hildebrand." Walter stopped walking and said, "Well, there she is…..*The Federico.*"

"Wow, that's quite some ship," said Steve, as he slowly pulled down his aviator glasses.

"Yes it is," said Walter smiling. "And now I want to introduce you to your only passenger and the owner."

Walter called out loudly, "Elizabeth, could you please come up to the deck."

She came up from the galley, peeked out and said, "Hi, Uncle Walter. I guess this is the captain of my ship?"

"Steve Weisen…meet Elizabeth Hildebrand," Walter gestured toward Liz.

As Liz walked out onto the deck, Steve was not prepared for what he saw.

"Hello, Steve," Liz said.

Liz stood up on deck wearing a nautical-themed outfit that hugged her in all the right places, complete with a captain's hat tilted to the side. He stood there with his mouth wide open and didn't realize his glasses had slid down from his nose and clattered onto the deck of the pier.

"Steve…it's customary to say hello back." Walter smiled as he said that.

Steve also started his security firm. In the United States, it was called the Weisen Security Company, and Romanesque Security Company for all of Europe, Asia, and Africa. He put together a team that previously had military training, including being proficient with most weapons. Men or women with any helicopter experience was a plus. Each went through a rigorous three weeks of specialty preparation. They were also well paid during this period.

So far, only one individual did not work out, and he left the group. Over a twelve-month period, Steve had assembled almost fifty members that covered seven states in the United States and another thirty-five members in Europe and Africa. Word got around of his operation, and he now was in high demand. He also developed four key team members that were responsible for the training.

Ernie Slater was an exCIA operative. He developed his skill during the Vietnam War era when you needed someone to set up electronic surveillance on individuals. Ernie's specialty was to monitor high-profile military individuals. His other specialty was a sniper and detonation expert. Each of his surveillance operations was successful. As a result, when he decided to go into private practice, the U.S. Government still used him occasionally as a contractor. He was even allowed to keep his *Crypto* clearance. Ernie worked for the U.S. Government, all over the world. His cover was as a news correspondent for a major newspaper in the United States.

He finally figured out that the constant traveling was taking its toll and he stopped working for the Government. However, he still kept the contacts he'd collected over the past twenty years. Before he left the service, as one of his last assignments, he was asked to teach classes at a U.S. Army post in Vilsec, Germany, to a select few officers from other NATO countries. That's how he met Rick Benedict.

Ernie stood about five feet eleven, with blond hair that never seemed to need combing. He had a boyish face, which gave him an advantage sometimes. He had his own business called Slater and Slater, Inc. He was a one-man show as far as his business was concerned. However, he decided that by having two names, it appeared he had a much larger operation. He could choose which clients to take, and he never had any of them come to his office. He always met them either at their home, office or some out of the way place. He catered primarily to high-level people in organizations.

Soon, word got around of his abilities, and his business grew. He hired an assistant named Wilber Watkins. He needed someone to manage his business while he was out working on a case. He got himself a small office, which was used to take messages and pay bills – and keep track of Ernie since he was always working somewhere in the world. Wilbur used to be in Ernie's unit when he was in Vietnam, working as an account clerk at headquarters in Phai Tang, Vietnam.

Ernie's personal life was chaotic in that he had various short-term personal relationships. He had two joys in his life. He loved spending time at one of the local bars called *The Last Squadron*. It was mainly military men from the Vietnam era. His other form of relaxation was that he had two girlfriends in Macau at the Red Dragon Casino. His close friend, Victor Chen managed it.

Chapter

18

Rick went up to the cockpit and said, "Del, let's turn around and go back to Providence. The trip is canceled temporarily."

Rick came back to where Liz was sitting, his face drawn, and tears streaming down his face. He sat down and held her in his arms.

"Darling, I have some bad news for you," Rick said, as tears were running down his face.

"What is it, Rick? You're scaring me," Liz said alarmed.

"That was Walter on the phone," Rick said solemnly. "My father, Jacob… is dead."

"What...What happened?" Liz asked.

Rick explained briefly, what Walter told him and said, "Walter wants us to cancel this trip and come back to his house. He said he would explain more at that time."

"Oh my gosh….this is terrible!" Liz said crying into Rick's arms.

Rick and Liz landed at the T. F. Green Airport in Warwick, Rhode Island. Duncan was waiting for them at their hangar. Rick, Liz, and Del saw Duncan, and without saying a word, they all got into the car. Duncan drove them to Walter's house, and all Rick could think of was, *I miss him so much and I never even got to say… goodbye.* As they drove there, they looked at each other and only had facial expressions, which said more than words. They drove up to the large oversized wrought iron gates and slowly drove up the driveway towards the house.

I remember when my father had those electronic gates installed, so he didn't have to sit out at the small guardhouse every day, Rick thought.

I also remember coming through those same gates for many years, not knowing that Jacob was my biological father.

As they stopped in front of the steps to Walter's house, Duncan quickly got out, held the doors open, and said, "I am so sorry for your loss, Rick."

"Thanks, Duncan," Rick said and continued walking up the steps, holding Liz's hand ever so tightly.

Walter came out to meet Rick and Liz and said, "I'm so sorry to be the bearer of bad news, Rick. He was one of my closest friends, and I will miss him dearly."

"Thanks, Walter," Rick said, as they hugged each other, and both had tears running down their cheeks.

They walked into the house and into the library.

Walter said somberly. "I have seen first-hand some of the cruelties of war, and I was a very lucky person to have survived. I never shed a tear for any of my friends that were in the concentration camp with me, because we did not have time to mourn. However, *this* is the cruelest thing, and I'm not sure I will ever get over losing my friend….Jacob."

Liz rushed over to her mother, Hilda and hugged her.

"I'm so sorry, Mother," Liz said trying to comfort her. "I know you've been through a lot in your lifetime. I was so happy when you were able to get a second chance in life when you married Jacob."

"Thank you, Elizabeth," Hilda said, with tears running down her face. "We both survived a terrible war, and I guess it was just not meant to be."

"Oh, don't say that," Liz said to her. "You know you can always come out and live on the ranch with us. You wouldn't have to do anything special, except baking the occasional Bundt cake for us," trying to add some levity to the situation, but it didn't seem to be working.

Later that day Steve arrived and gave his men instructions, "I want two people posted inside the front gate; two people by the back gate and the rest come with me."

The men positioned themselves strategically inside as well as outside and around Walter's main house. Each had a full unobstructed view of their area, and each was armed. Steve drove the rest of the men to the main house. Walter walked out to meet them.

"Hello Steve…..men," Walter said. "Thank you all for coming on such short notice.

"I'm sorry to be here under these circumstances," Steve replied. "But we're here so that nothing else happens to you or your family."

"Ernie is also here as well," Walter said. "Come into the house, when you're ready."

"Just give me ten minutes," Steve said, as he ran off in the direction of the front gate.

Chapter

19

They were all sitting at the large conference room table in Walter's study, somber because of the recent events.

After a moment of silence, Walter spoke, "Here is what I've been able to piece together so far." He explained about the new tenant in his building, the new llama ranch in Chile, the hacking of the company's database, and now the death of Jacob.

"It appears that in each of these instances, Rancagua, Chile, keeps coming up," Walter said. "To further add to this mystery, Leonard Schultz's family crypt was moved to Chile!

I know I've made some enemies in the past, Walter thought. *However, now suddenly they are invading my very home, family as well as my business.*

"Fred, I'd like you to perform a more in-depth look into Jason Segal, the new person that moved into my building," said Walter, "because he happened to come from Rancagua. We need to find out who moved the entire family crypt of Leonard Schultz to Chile. Lastly, find out what you can, on Arturo Souza, who is the new owner of a llama ranch and wants to sell Mustafa his wool. Like I indicated before, there are far *too* many things happening out of Chile."

"Whew, that's a tall order," Fred said.

"Ernie, I would like you to take a trip to Rancagua, Chile, and see what you can find out," Walter said. "Start with the *Mr. Belvedere Restaurant.* Even go to the cemetery and see where Leonard family crypt is located."

"I'd like to have some of Steve's people come with me so that we can cover more ground," Ernie said.

"Steve, have you got several people that can help Ernie with this?" Walter asked.

"I do," Steve, answered.

"Fred will be here for several days, so you may call him if you need him to access any information," Walter said.

"What can *we* do to help in this situation?" asked Rick. "I have my plane here, and I can fly Ernie and Steve's people over there."

"Yes. Let's do that," Walter said coolly.

"What can *I* do to help out?" Liz asked.

"Liz....I would like you to take care of Hilda, your mother," Walter said. "Right now she is very fragile and will need some time."

"I agree, but since everybody is going to be gone," Liz said, "I'd like a weapon in case we have problems."

"I can take care of that, Liz," Duncan said. "I'll be right back," and he left to go to his house.

Duncan came back a few minutes later brandishing a 9mm Parabellum Glock pistol and said, "This should keep you safe. It has a fifteen-round clip and here are two additional clips."

"Thanks, Duncan," Liz smiled. "Now I feel safe."

"One other thing," Walter said, turning to Steve. "I think we should set up more surveillance cameras around the property. Buy all the cameras you need. We'll set up a special room in this house to monitor everything and record all movements. Lastly, Rick and Liz, I want you to call all of your people at your businesses, and tell them to be on the lookout for *anything* suspicious. But don't scare them."

"We will do that right now," Liz said.

"Steve. Can you have at least one security person at each of Liz's and my restaurants, without telling the managers what we are doing?" Walter asked.

"Yes, I can do that," Steve replied.

"I also have a hunch," Walter said, "and I could be wrong, that whoever is pulling these *strings* is also *very* familiar with all of our business interests."

The next day, Fred called Walter from his headquarters office and said, "Well, I've destroyed all of the one hundred and seventy-four firewalls, and I did find the *bug* that had been planted. But like I said before, it was easy."

"Perhaps, too easy," Walter said under his breath.

Chapter

20

Walter was now concerned for the welfare of everyone that was close to him. He sat at his desk trying to make sense out of all it......and he was drawing a blank. As he looked out of his window behind his desk, he noticed it was getting darker, and the security lights finally came on.

He called Aki and said, "I am in need of your unique skills. Can you come up to the house, please?"

"Yes, Mr. Donleavy, I will be right over," Aki responded.

As Aki drove the golf cart over to Walter's house, he passed the twelve-car garage behind the house. He noticed a small beam of light weaving up and down. He stopped the golf cart and cautiously made his way to one of the windows and looked in. He saw a dark shadow moving around apparently looking for something. Aki made his way inside running noiselessly and was on top of the individual in seconds.

The intruder was out cold, so Aki picked him up, carried him out and sat him in the golf cart and continued driving to the front of Walter's house. He pulled him off the golf cart, carried him up the four steps to the front door, and laid him down on the steps and rang the doorbell.

"Mr. Donleavy," Aki said, "I caught this man rummaging around in your garage. Do you know him?"

"Turn him over in the light so that I can see him better," Walter said.

As he turned him over, the individual started to stir and said, "Where am I?"

"Who are you and what are you doing on my property?"

Walter asked loudly.

"I don't have to talk to you!" he said arrogantly, still laying on the steps.

"*Yes*, you do, and *yes* you will," Walter said abruptly as he looked at Aki.

Aki pinched a nerve on his neck, and immediately the man yelled.

"Hey. You can't torture me. I have rights!" he yelled back, still sitting on the ground.

"You're on *my* property and as far as I'm concerned...you have *no* rights," Walter said. "I can have you *shot* and bury you *anywhere* on my five thousand acres, and nobody will ever find you! Now tell me what you're doing here, or I'll have my friend cripple you so badly, you'll wish you were dead.....or beg for a bullet."

Aki leaned over and again pinched the nerve on his neck, and again he shouted out in pain.

"I suggest you tell Mr. Donleavy what he wants to know," Aki said. "If I keep pinching this nerve, at some point you'll stop screaming because you think it does not hurt anymore. Except that from your waist down, you will lose all feeling – forever. Think about living in a wheelchair for the rest of your life. You have only precious seconds to tell him what he wants to know."

"What's your name?" Walter demanded.

He looked around, confused and finally said, "Hank Douglas.

Duncan leaned over him, searched him, found a wallet in his pocket, and gave it to Walter.

"Hey, you can't take that," Douglas yelled out, trying to reach for his wallet.

"Do you see that gentleman next to you?" Walter asked. "If I tell him to, he can break both your arms and both your legs and break your jaw. The good thing is that you won't feel the pain until you wake up in the hospital in a full body cast. However, the bad thing is that when you *do* finally wake up, you will be in excruciating pain. Now stop acting stupid!"

The intruder looked over at Aki and started to panic. "All right...all right," he said.

Walter looked at his wallet and remarked, "Why does your driver's license say, Joseph Jenkins? Think before you speak, because if I don't like the answer....nobody will ever see you again."

"Yes, I'm Joseph Jenkins," he said embarrassed that he'd been caught as he rubbed his neck muscles.

"How did you get onto my estate?" Walter asked him.

"That was easy," he said, suddenly sounding almost cheerful. "I drive a van, which I parked right next to your fence. I get on top of my van roof and just jumped over."

"How were you going to get back *over* the fence once you found what you were going steal?" asked Walter.

"That's also easy," he said. "Everybody always has a ladder I can use."

"You still haven't explained what you're doing here?" Walter said viciously.

He hesitated, looked at Aki, but finally said, "I figured that a place this big, you can afford a few "lost" tools here and there, and that's all. Anybody that has a twelve-car garage has got to have some great tools I could steal and sell at a swap meet."

"Are you kidding me? A common thief!" Walter said loudly.

By this time, the thief was standing up and dusting himself off. Walter walked over to him with clenched teeth and, with all his might, punched him right in the face. You could hear cartilage break as he fell backward onto the gravel road. Blood was running out of his nose, as he lay there not moving.

"Wow, Walter," Rick exclaimed. "I didn't know you had it in you."

"There are still things that you do not know about me, Rick," Walter said as he winked at him.

That was one special punch, Duncan thought.

"Duncan, tie him up and call the police...again," Walter said. "I will be in to press charges in the morning."

"I'll take care of it, Mr. Donleavy," Duncan said as he grabbed the intruder. *How do you get blood off of white rocks*, he wondered.

Chapter

21

Soon the police came, and Duncan let them in the front gate.

"This is becoming a habit," said the police officer.

"I hope this *doesn't* become a regular requirement," Duncan said. "He's over here," pointing to the steps.

"Oh, yes....Mr. Jenkins," the officer, said walking towards him. "He's a regular with us. He should have a van parked around here somewhere. I'll have it towed to impound."

"Joseph, I do not want to see you here *ever* again!" Duncan said. "I mean *never* again. The next time I may just shoot first and ask questions later."

"I assume you have a permit for those?" the officer asked, pointing to his weapons.

"Absolutely!" Duncan said as he pulled out his permit.

"Wow. An international gun permit" said the officer. "You don't see many of those."

Duncan took back his card, feeling very proud, and said, "I fly all over the world as security for Mr. Donleavy."

In Aki's previous job in his younger days, he was responsible for the life of a very powerful real estate developer in Kyoto, Japan. Aki's father and his father before him were all ninjas and samurai warriors, with only one goal in life, and that was to protect. He had trained in all of the martial art techniques of the Ninja assassin. He went on to learn all of the secrets of the Samurai warrior. He used his deadly skills only on rare occasions but was ready, if necessary.

His Master had passed away, and after some time, the family didn't see a need for his services, so he was no longer obligated to serve the family. His previous Master also had a small Kobe beef ranch outside of Kyoto, and he began to appreciate how they raised them. He quickly found that he liked ranching. He now had a *new* Master to protect who had similar ideas. He liked that. Some Ninjas were hired to act as bodyguards for the very wealthy executives of companies, as well as to protect the family.

Walter had brought Aki Watanabe, and his wife Tomichi came over from Japan in 1975. He'd met him at a trade fair when Walter was going to purchase more live Kobe beef cows to support his own two restaurants. He invited Aki to lunch to discuss his plans and to make him an offer. Aki was surprised, and curious at the same time, but listened.

"I currently have about fifty head of Kobe cattle," Walter said. "Many of my patrons revere my Kobe beef dinners. I serve it at my two restaurants, and it has always been a big hit. Your compensation will be very good, and you can bring your family with you. You will have your own house and can come and go as you please."

Aki was surprised with such an extremely generous offer from a man he had just met. This actually came at an opportune time in Aki's life, since his parents had both passed away, his wife, Tomichi was an orphan, and they had no brothers or sisters.

Walter leaned forward and said, "Aki, I'm not hiring you only to manage my cattle. I want you to be a long-term partner. I realized long ago that a paycheck is *not* what drives good men. To achieve bigger things, you have to give them an opportunity to grow. You and I will do great things together."

"Money is not necessarily a motivator for me," said Aki.

"I realized that when I first met you," said Walter. "For me to be successful, I need someone who is the best. Now, you may say there are others that are better than you are. I would have to disagree – because I have the best sitting in front of me right now. I just have one basic rule. I always want to know the truth. Whether it's good news or bad news, I still want to know. If it's bad, let me know as soon as possible so we can fix the problem.

Please do not be afraid to make mistakes. We all make them, but many people make the *bigger* mistake of not learning, or try to hide from them."

Chapter

22

The next morning, Rick flew with Ernie and two of Steve's security people to Rancagua, Chile. They landed at the Santiago Airport, with no problems. They went through Customs and then went directly to rent a large van.

"Del. You stay with the plane, get it fueled up just in case we have to leave in a hurry," Rick said.

"I'll take care of it Rick," Del replied, wishing he could go with them.

"Ernie, what are we going to do for some firepower?" asked Rick.

"Not to worry, Rick," Ernie said grinning as if he just swallowed a canary. "A friend of mine is going to meet us at our motel as soon as I call him and tell him which place. Right now let's go to the *Mr. Belvedere Restaurant*, the place Fred said had made those calls to Claus before he did a swan dive out of the twelfth-floor window."

They all drove over to the *Mr. Belvedere Restaurant*. As they walked in, they were met with cold stares from almost everyone, including from the bartender.

Ernie casually walked up to the man behind the bar and asked, "How about a beer for me and my friends?"

"Si, senor," the bartender said, curious as to why they were here. He sat the beers down in front of each of the men and walked away.

"Excuse me," Ernie said. "Do you have a phone I could use? I have a sick mother, and I have to check in on her from time to time."

"Si, we have a pay phone on the wall close to the bathroom," he said, as he pointed in the direction where the bathroom is located.

"Be right back, fellas," Ernie said, as he walked over to the pay phone on the wall. He wrote down the phone number, picked the lock on the box, placed a tiny microchip inside, and closed up the box. "I'm glad you're feeling better, Mother. I'll talk to you soon," he said and walked back to the bar.

"Do many people use that phone?" Ernie asked as he walked back to the bar.

The bartender didn't answer but made a gesture with his eyes to six, very large and ugly guys that were sitting at a table in the corner. They casually walked over and stood behind Ernie.

"Why do you ask so many questions, senor?" asked one of the men, in a condescending voice.

Ernie turned to him and said, "I don't see that it is any of your business."

Suddenly the man pulled out a *facon*, a foot-long knife used primarily in the field. With clenched teeth that were brown and stained, looking as if they hadn't seen a toothbrush since he was born, tried to rush Ernie.

Ernie easily sidestepped him and hit him in the gut hard, which made him drop his knife. He doubled up obviously in pain as all the air went out of him, and he dropped to the floor. The bartender watched all of this and was alarmed. He started reaching for something behind the bar. Rick caught that movement out of the corner of his eye, grabbed him by his shirt, and almost pulled him over the top of the bar.

"You may not realize this, friend," Rick said, "but I just saved your life." Rick continued holding onto the bartender's shirt, who now panicked, frantically trying to get away.

Pete and Thomas took care of the other four men that tried to rush them.

"Now, I'm going to ask you again!" Ernie turned around, facing the bartender, while Rick was still holding onto his shirt, and asked loudly, "Do many people use that phone?"

"I'll bet they have an office of some type with a phone in there," Rick said.

"That's a good idea," Ernie said. "Where *is* your office?"

The bartender pointed to the left side of the building, still trembling.

Ernie then grabbed the bartender from Rick and said, "Show me where it is!"

They walked to a door that said "PRIVADO," opened it, and walked in.

"This is obviously *not* the bartender's office," Ernie remarked as he looked around. There was a large oak desk, which cried out *expensive*. "Hold on to him outside for me, Rick," Ernie said.

Ernie went in and closed the door behind him. On the desk were a few knick-knack statues and four telephones. As he got closer to the desk, he noticed three of the phones had a phone number on the dial. He checked to see if they all had a dial tone and he took each apart, put a small microchip, or bug into the handset and put it back in its cradle. He also jotted down all the phone numbers. The fourth phone was blue, but had no visible phone number on the dial. He went to the blue phone, picked up the phone, and listened.

Within a few seconds, a voice came on and said, "Vilosco, why are you calling me?"

Ernie didn't answer the person, listened for a moment, and put the phone down gently back in its cradle. *That voice sounds familiar*, he thought. *The voice is so clear, and I'm sure I've heard it before*. Ernie looked around, but nothing stood out that interested him.

Ernie came out of the office and said, "Let's get outta here fellas. I have a feeling we're going to have visitors soon."

Rick let the bartender go when they were by the front door. They hurriedly left the restaurant, got in their van and took off, as if they were being chased.

"Did you find out anything in his office?" asked Rick.

"He had four phones in that office," Ernie said. "What's peculiar was the one that was blue with no number on the dial. But, when I picked up the handset, it immediately connected to someone, and a voice came over the phone, that I know I've heard before."

"No kiddin," Rick said surprised.

"It's been my experience that it's probably connected to some high-level person in the police department," Thomas said. "Or it was someone very special or powerful that was well connected to some organization."

"I have to agree with Thomas about that," Ernie said.

"The other phone numbers you jotted down," Rick asked. "Are you going to track those down?"

"I have a little device that allows me to track several hundred phone numbers at once," Ernie said. "Let's get to a hotel or motel so that I can set up my surveillance system. I also think we should get something to eat. I would stay away from the local water and either drink imported beer or a soda. I'm also going to call my friend to come see us."

As soon as they left, Vilosco, the bartender, went into the office and picked up the *blue* phone and said, "I just had four visitors come to your restaurant and beat up my friends, and then they left."

"What did they want?" he asked.

"I don't know. They didn't say," Vilosco, said panicking and perspiring. "One went into the office by himself, was in there for a few moments and then just left."

"You've never seen them before?" he asked.

"No, senor," Vilosco said.

There was a pause on the phone when the other individual asked, "Was one of them blond, around six feet tall, and wore a baseball hat?"

"Si, senor," Miguel quickly said.

"Thank you for calling me Vilosco."

It must be Ernie Slater, he thought. *How could he find me so quickly?*

"Hello Rolf," Arturo said, sounding cheerful. "How is my favorite financial advisor?"

"Hi Arturo," said Rolf. "What can I do for you?"

"Has anybody contacted you or anyone else in your company asking about me?" Arturo asked.

"No, not that I know of," Rolf said. "Should I be concerned?"

"Not at all. Just checking," Arturo said and hung up the phone.

I may have to step up my plans now, he thought.

Chapter

23

Ernie drove to a part of town that looked like it had been in a war. The houses looked very dilapidated, with trash that hadn't been picked up in a while. They drove into the parking lot of a small, multi-colored motel with doors to match. Ernie checked them into one room because it was more for setting up a surveillance post.

"Pete, you and Thomas scout around the outside of this building," Ernie said, "and make sure we have some extra exits in case we have to leave suddenly."

"How about if I go out and get some food for us all?" Rick said.

"That's a good idea," Ernie said. "Meanwhile, I'll connect with Fred and see if he's found out anything new."

"Hi Fred," Ernie said. "Anything new?"

"I checked further and found the restaurant, *Mr. Belvedere* has four phone numbers," Fred said.

"I found that out also," Ernie said, "but that doesn't include the payphone close to the mens room."

"One number is kind of interesting," Fred said, "because it only directly connects to one other phone number. And that's located in the *Adolpho Vincenti Vineyards* in Rancagua, Chile."

"That *is* interesting," Ernie said. "I guess that will be my second stop tomorrow morning. See what you can find out about the owner of the place."

"Will do," Fred said and hung up.

"Tomorrow morning, fellas, we're going to go to *Palmyra Cemetery* first, which happens to be in Rancagua," Ernie said.

"Then we'll go to the *Adolpho Vincenti Vineyards*. It seems that the blue phone only connects to that place. See if you guys can get a little shut-eye. It's going to be a busy day tomorrow."

Fred spent the better part of that day researching those two items. After spending an exhausting amount of time and almost ready to stop for the day, he started to see a common thread that connected events. Fred got so excited he almost fell out of his chair.

"Walter!" Fred exclaimed loudly. "I think I found the connection!"

Pete Lindquist was in the service with Steve Weisen. He had already served fifteen years in the Marines when he was assigned to a tank battalion and deployed to the Desert Storm conflict. He was stationed in Kuwait along with other tank drivers holding off the invaders. It was a short tour, and he was almost shipped back to the U.S. along with some of the other equipment.

Pete was hoping for a longer tour of duty because he knew that the insurgents were just biding their time. His last assignment was to train the Kuwaiti Army to drive the tanks that the United States sold them. Because of his rank as a Master Sergeant, the military discharged him in Kuwait, but he stayed on and hired on as a civilian contractor. He was there an extra year, made a lot of money, and thought about settling down in Saudi Arabia. His contract had run out, so he decided to go back stateside.

He wandered around in Texas, working odd jobs, but he had that constant yearning to reenlist in the military. He happened to have lunch at a bar that other service members frequented and overheard a conversation about a security company being assembled. He turned around and recognized Steve Weisen.

"I thought I recognized that voice," Pete said smiling and turned to face him.

"Well, I'll be. Pete, how are you?" Steve asked

"I couldn't help but overhear about you are starting up a security service," Pete said.

"Yes, are you interested?" Steve asked.

"Tell me some more about it," Pete said.

Steve and Pete talked for quite a while and the longer they talked, the more Pete felt that he'd found a *home*.

After a brief interview with Steve, Pete said, "I'm in as long as this does not become a desk job."

"Don't worry about that," Steve said. "I wouldn't waste your talents behind a desk."

"I'm glad we talked," Steve said. "I'm going to build the best security team in the world."

Thomas Harrington worked for Steve Weisen as part of Weisen Security. He, along with several security agents, had all known either Steve or Ernie and served with them in the military. After he left the military, he got a job as a skydiving instructor in Palm Springs, California. He took on the additional job as a hot air balloon navigator for sightseeing customers. He left that job because some of his clients were getting belligerent and drunk. One person almost fell overboard, and the only way he knew to stop him was to punch him so he would quiet down.

When they landed, the client had gone over to the manager complaining and said, "He punched me, and I want him fired!"

The manager didn't know what else to do, so he said to Thomas, "Sorry, but I've got to let you go."

"That's no problem," Thomas said. "Being up in the air at a thousand feet was no place to get drunk and kill yourself. I quit! You can take your balloons and stick em where the sun don't shine."

"Good riddance," the drunk client said.

Thomas heard that, dropped his jacket on the field, turned around and walked up to him and said, "If you weren't so stupid, you would realize that I just saved your life up there! Next time you won't be so lucky!"

He picked up his jacket and left.

Chapter

24

"When I lay this out like a timeline, you'll see some interesting things show up," Fred said. He went to Walter's white-board and created a timeline for the events that connected everything. "Walter, you can see at a glance that this series of events was well thought out by the individual.

"Item 1, starting with when Leonard died.

"Item 2, a few months later Leonard's house was sold and the money went into a trust held by a financial institution in Frankfurt, Germany.

"Item 3, a month after that, Leonard's entire family crypt was completely moved to *Palmyra Cemetery*, which is in Rancagua, Chile.

"Item 4, four months later, a person named Arturo Souza buys the *Adolpho Vincenti Vineyard* which is located….in Rancagua, Chile.

"Item 5, several months after that, the same Arturo Souza bought the *Santa Rita llama Ranch*, located in Maipo Valley, which also happens to be…..in Chile.

"Item 6, your new tenant, Jason Segal who moved into your building, happened to also come from somewhere…..in Chile.

"Item 7, during this same time, you hired Claus Livingston as your CFO, who happened to have worked *directly* for Leonard Schultz at one time.

"Item 8, a month later, after your database was hacked and Claus killed himself, we found out that at the time, he was talking to somebody at the *Mr. Belvedere Restaurant*, which happens to be in…..Rancagua, Chile.

"Item 9, Ernie found a telephone that has a direct line to the *Adolpho Vincenti Vineyard*, which happens to be in Chile, and Arturo Souza is the owner of that winery.

"Item 10, here is one last piece of this puzzle," Fred said triumphantly. "It might be a coincidence, but the case of wine that killed Jacob – was also a wine from the *Adolpho Vincenti* Vineyards, which is made in.....Chile."

When Walter heard what Fred just told him, he started to pace back and forth in deep thought.

"This is unbelievable!" Walter remarked.

He finally turned back to Fred and said, "One more thing. Check to see if there were any private flights directly from Chile, especially from an airport close to Rancagua, which have landed at the T. F. Green Airport in Warwick, Rhode Island within the last two weeks. I have a hunch."

After searching for about thirty minutes, Fred finally said, "I actually found several flights. However, I only found *one* with the name of Arturo Souza, who flew in just two days before Jacob was killed."

"That's what I thought," Walter said. "Now it all makes sense!"

"What are you talking about?" Fred asked.

"I don't think Leonard is dead at all!" Walter said aloud. "Arturo Souza and Leonard Schultz are *one* and the *same* person!"

"Are you serious?" Fred said as if lightning hit him.

"As serious as a heart attack!" Walter said.

Walter was very excited to find all these things out, but now he had to create a plan to stop this *roller-coaster* ride.

Walter said, "Let's call Ernie and see if he can firm up who paid to have the crypt moved to Chile."

"I can probably find that out," Fred said.

A few minutes later, Fred asked Walter, "Do you remember a name like Rolf Freiberg from Frankfurt, Germany?"

"Yes, I do remember the name," Walter said.

"He was instrumental in handling the purchase of the vineyard and llama ranch in Rancagua for Arturo," Fred said. "This might also prove that Leonard and Arturo are the same person."

"I think you are on the right track," Walter said.

"Also, I was able to access Leonard's past income tax returns," Fred said. "You'll never guess who filled it out for him?"

"Who would that be?" Walter asked.

"Rolf Freiburg of Frankfurt Financial," said Fred. "Another coincidence?"

"I think not!" Walter said annoyed. "Let's call Ernie and alert him to this new information."

Chapter

25

Ernie dialed Fred, and after several rings, Ernie said, "Hello Fred. Anything new? We're on our way to the Palmyra Cemetery."

"Yes, actually," Fred said. "Walter and I feel that Arturo Souza, who owns the *Adolpho Vincenti Vineyards in Rancagua and* the *Santa Rita Ranch in Maipo Valley, is actually*.... Leonard Schultz."

"I knew I heard that voice before!" Ernie exclaimed. "I just knew it!"

"What do you mean, *you thought so*?" Walter asked.

"Remember when I said a voice came on the phone when I picked up the handset from the blue phone at that restaurant in town?" Ernie said, gushing with excitement.

"Yes," Walter said, listening intently.

"Well, now it's confirmed!" Ernie said. "I still want to go to the cemetery and see what we can find out. Then we'll drive over to the *Adolpho Vincenti Vineyards* and just casually walk into the wine tasting room. Rick or I won't go in because Leonard knows what we looks like today. I'll send in Thomas and Pete since I don't think he knows them."

"Ernie, if it is confirmed that it's Leonard....then don't do anything for the moment," Walter said. "I have to handle this..... myself," and stood there, head down, in deep thought.

"Okay, Walter," Ernie said curiously.

As Walter walked towards his study, Fred asked, "Is there anything else you want me to do?"

"Just one last thing, Fred," Walter said excitedly. "If you perform a search for Arturo Souza, I don't think you'll find anything on him past the last few years."

"Let's find out," Fred said. Over the next few minutes, he searched various databases.

"I think this is interesting," Fred said. "I think you're correct.

However, here is the curious part. The real Arturo died about two years ago. That was about the same time Leonard died. In fact, here is a picture of the real Arturo. This person is obviously around eighty years old, is very short and a little on the heavy side. He also died in a car crash while he was on vacation in Ecuador."

"Fantastic, Fred!" Walter said elated with this new information.

"I think that's it for now Fred. Thanks for all your help," he said and continued walking into his study.

Fred watched Walter walk over to his desk and sat down in his chair. *I can only guess what he's feeling*, he thought. *He is a very difficult and complex man to read.*

Ernie drove to the *Palmyra Cemetery*. It was not large, but most of the gravesites had very elaborate carved granite headstones. They drove in, trying to find someone who could direct them to the Schultz family crypt. He spotted a sign that said LA OFICINA, pointing to a small building with parking in the front.

Ernie and Rick walked in and asked, "Can you direct me to the Leonard Schultz family Crypt?"

"Yes, I can," said the caretaker. "It's at the end of this road. You can't miss it. It's the biggest structure in our cemetery."

"I'm told it is a magnificent structure," Ernie said. "Can you tell me who built it?"

"Yes," the caretaker said. "In fact, here is one of their business cards."

The card read,

> *Majestic Stone Masons, specializing in building family crypts. Offices in Santiago, Chile; Frankfurt, Germany; Orlando, Florida, and Palm Springs, California.*

"Thanks very much," Ernie said and left.

They drove to the end of the road, and as they neared the crypt, all were awestruck at how beautiful and large the structure was.

"That is enormous!" Rick said. "It must have cost a fortune to have it moved from Gstaad stone by stone and having it shipped about eight thousand miles away to Rancagua, Chile!"

"When you have a *lot* of money," Ernie said, "and you have nobody to leave your money to, you're going to spend it somewhat frivolously."

"That makes sense…I guess," Rick said.

Chapter

26

I have so much still to do, Arturo thought. *Those little things can not derail me.*

He called his pilot Gaspar and said, "I want to fly to San Ignacio, Bolivia. I want to see a llama ranch located near there."

"We can leave tomorrow as early as you like, Mr. Souza," Gaspar said.

"Good. From there I want to fly to Tel Aviv, Israel," Arturo, said. "There is a rug merchant that sells high-quality carpets. I may try to buy that company. If I like what I see, I'll make them an offer they can't refuse."

"Okay, Mr. Souza," Gaspar said.

Ernie still wanted to see Arturo Souza and at least get a picture of how he looked now.

"I'm still beside myself," Ernie said, "that Arturo and Leonard might be the same person."

"I'm as amazed as you are. But I agree, we should settle this," Rick said. "We've come this far, and I would also like to see what he looks like now. Don't forget what Walter said the last time we spoke to him. He said..... *I have to handle this myself.*"

"Yeah, he did say that," Ernie said. "And I'm afraid I think I know what he means by that."

"Fred, one other thing before you pack up," Walter said. "The flight that you found that Arturo took to Providence had a pilot. I'm guessing it was a private plane. Find out his name and anything else you can find out about him. Maybe someone is looking for him......and he doesn't want to be found."

"Okay," Fred said, wondering where this was going to lead.

It was now around nine o'clock at night as Ernie, and his group all headed back to the motel to regroup. A little later, there was a knock on the door. Ernie went to see who it was as he peeked through the window.

"Well, there is a sorry sight if I've ever seen one," Ernie said, as he opened the door, smiling and giving a big bear hug to his friend.

"Hello Ernie," he said. "How are you, my friend?" He plunked down a nondescript duffle bag on one of the beds.

"Doing well Michael," Ernie said. "I want to introduce you to my friends," as they shook hands with them.

"Hi fellas," he said happily.

"This guy was with me in Vietnam," Ernie said proudly. "He is the guy that everybody wanted to have as a friend. He was a quartermaster in Saigon working for the 101st Airborne Division. Michael has helped me out so many times. When you're in the jungle fighting for your life, you tend to lose things. This guy could get you almost anything you wanted."

"Now that's the kind of friend that you want to keep forever," Rick said smiling.

"His specialty is weapons…of any type," Ernie said. "I would typically carry at least four .45 caliber pistols and about twenty magazines. I would go through them like changing socks. Yeah, those were the good old days, when you didn't have to fill out requisition forms. Anyway, this is Michael."

"It's a pleasure to meet you all," Michael said. "However, I think he embellishes a little too much. He hasn't told you about how he has helped me out of some sticky jams."

"Okay, enough with the war stories," Ernie said sounding serious, "I'm getting all misty. What have you got for me, besides my guns?"

"This guy, Arturo Souza has about twenty to thirty guards around him at all times," Michael said. "He has twelve-foot high chain-link fencing with two rows of razor-sharp concertina wiring covering the top. The kicker is that most of the time it is electrified."

"Around the entire property?" Ernie asked.

"No," Michael said. "Just around the property that surrounds his house, tennis courts, swimming pool and a huge oversized garage, which sits on about two acres."

"What about access points?" Ernie asked.

"He has a double gate in the front entrance with four guards," Michael said. "He also has a back exit gate and several guards posted there as well."

"No offense, but how reliable is your information?" Rick asked.

"None taken," Michael, remarked, "Because you see...I work there part time picking the grapes during harvest time."

Ernie had to chuckle and said, "Michael, you're a gem. When we get through with all of this, you, Pete and Thomas are going to be my guests at the *Red Dragon Casino and Resort* in Macau. Rick... you can't come because you already have a great gal waiting for you at home."

"I don't know....this Macau thing sounds kinda interesting....... and lots of fun," Rick said, laughing. "Yeah, I guess you're right."

"Let's check in with Walter and see if there is anything new," Ernie said.

"Yeah, that's a good idea," Rick said. "Maybe they found out what drove Arturo or Leonard to do this."

Ernie dialed the phone. "Hi Walter," he said. "We went to the cemetery and saw the crypt for Leonard's family. I must tell you... it's huge. We also got the name of the company that took it apart in Gstaad and put it back together in Rancagua. The company name is *Majestic Stone Masons*, and they specialize in building a family crypt. Coincidentally, they have an office in Santiago, Chile, and of course in Frankfurt, Germany."

"Yes. Fred also happened to find that out," Walter said, "as he was going through Leonard's financial documents and tax filings."

"I have a friend here, who gave us some additional info about Arturo's house and guards," Ernie said.

"Good. I had Fred track down Arturo's pilot, which also gives us his flight plans," Walter said. "They took off for Bolivia and the San Ignacio Airport."

"Then you wouldn't mind if we did something to the vineyard and his outer buildings?" Ernie asked, hoping he would say yes.

"No! I don't mind at all!" Walter said enthusiastically. "Burn it all down, in memory of my friend….Jacob." *I suspect it was probably his pilot Gaspar, that set the bomb and dropped off the wine at my doorstep*, he thought.

Ernie looked up at Michael and asked, "Do any of your friends stay or live on the property?"

"No. The workers all have their own places to live in," Michael said. "What are you thinking?"

"A few well-placed large Molotov-like cocktails ought to do the trick," Ernie said. "A little wind will do the rest. One other thing. Can you get ahold of a chopper?"

"Yes. That's no problem," Michael said smiling. "I don't even have to steal it…because it's already mine and it's not very far from here."

"Well, boys," Ernie said happily, "tonight they'll see this fire from twenty thousand feet."

"Wait a minute. If Arturo is heading to Bolivia," Rick said, "he may be going after my St. Augustine Ranch in San Ignacio."

"That's possible," Ernie said. "I suggest you alert them and maybe get over there yourself. I'll take care of things here. When you're complete, swing by here and pick us up."

Chapter

27

Rick called Lance Driscoll, his new general manager of the St. Augustine Ranch.

"Hi Lance," Rick said. "I just want to alert you that you may have some unwelcome guests at the ranch. I don't have time to explain right now."

"Okay, but what am I looking at?" Lance asked.

"I'm not sure, but call up one of the security companies we talked about in the past and get about ten men with weapons out to the ranch right away."

"Okay, I can do that!" Lance said.

"Is there a lot of wool ready to be shipped?" asked Rick.

"Yes, there is," Lance, said. "We were going to ship in a few days."

"That's what I was afraid of," Rick said with a worried look on his face. "That wool needs to be protected. Post extra guards around that area. Next, see if you can herd all the llamas out to another area of the property, so they don't get hurt.......or killed. It may be overkill, but I don't actually know what to expect. I just want to be ready for anything."

"I'll take care of that," Lance said. "Anything else?"

"Yes. Just make sure the guards are *all* armed," Rick said. "I'll see you soon." *There's something I was hoping would never happen,* he thought.

"Let's go, Del," Rick said. "We've got to get to my ranch in San Ignacio, in Bolivia as quickly as possible."

Lance Driscoll was your typical cowboy, with that same weathered-range look that Don Smith has. He stood about six-feet-two, with dark brown hair. He knew Don from both high school and college because they both played football. He was also a no-nonsense person. He understood the value of teamwork. He was not married at the time, so it worked out well for him to move to Bolivia. He was engaged for a short time, and for some reason, which he still doesn't quite understand, she took off with her brother to Alaska to work on the oil pipeline. Lance had a difficult time getting over that break-up.

He worked on several other cattle ranches in Texas, Wyoming, and Colorado. Rick had purchased two thousand head of cattle, which they were going to ship by rail to the Fort Collins area and ultimately to the Monarch Ranch. Lance was one of the wranglers who drove them to the railroad stockyard in Casper, Wyoming. That's where he met Don Smith for the second time. They got along well, and before he knew it, Don had offered him a job at the Monarch Ranch working for him.

Don Smith was born and raised in Colorado. He worked at the Monarch Ranch long before Rick purchased it. He earned a Master's degree from the University of Colorado in ecology and evolutionary biology. Don stood over six feet tall and wore his western hat like a badge of honor. He had that rugged, tanned face, with those special features that you see in television commercials inviting people to come out West and see the sights. He'd married Maureen, his college sweetheart, and they'd been together ever since. Don served two years as a drill sergeant at the El Toro Marine Base in California. He didn't re-enlist because it wasn't challenging enough, and he missed riding on the open range and sleeping under the stars.

As Rick was flying to his ranch in Bolivia, he had already worked out what he was going to do if they came and tried to create any havoc at all.

"Del, I know you have some firepower," Rick said. "I just realized that I've got to get to the ranch before I can get a weapon for me."

"I remember that Steve got an international license for Duncan to carry a firearm," Del said. "I think we should have Steve get us all a license like that."

"That's a great idea," Rick said.

Chapter

28

Michael drove Ernie and his partners to an area where he stored his chopper. He opened a small hangar door, and Ernie saw an old Hughes OH-6A Cayuse Helicopter that he used to fly himself in Vietnam.

"This takes me back," said Ernie, smiling from ear to ear, with his hands outstretched reminiscing in his mind when he flew one of these things on many missions in Vietnam.

"She is in great shape," Michael said with pride. "Please bring her back in one piece."

"I've lost a lot of things, my friend," Ernie said excitedly, "but a helicopter is *not* one of them. I need some large glass bottles, gasoline, and some rags."

"I can do better than that," Michael said, as he pulled back a tarp. "I have some napalm. I use it to clear large fields for other vintners."

"That's fantastic!" Ernie shouted out. "However, I want you to send me a bill for this stuff."

"Don't worry about that for now," Michael said.

"No, I'm serious," said Ernie, "because I know this stuff is expensive. Okay, men, let's load up."

Within a short time, the helicopter was loaded with napalm and was pushed out to an open area outside the hangar. Ernie got in and started the chopper up. The blades turned slowly as they came to life and finally picked up speed.

"Here are the coordinates for the vineyard," Michael said. "I'll wait for you here. Good luck, my friend."

Ernie took off and headed for the *Adolpho Vincenti Vineyards*. Pete and Thomas each sat behind him, ready to operate one of the M2 Browning .50 caliber machine guns in case of any problems.

"Okay, men. We're getting close, so get ready," Ernie said.

He turned off all outside lights so they would be difficult to see from the ground.

"Okay....here we go," Ernie said, as he shot out several bursts of napalm.

Everything became scorched in a matter of seconds. A few more bursts and the entire vineyard was ablaze.

"This is for you, Jacob," Ernie said softly. "Let's go and see the building where they process the grapes and wine room," and he veered to his left sharply.

"I don't think they'll be harvesting grapes this year...or any other year," Thomas said loudly over the sound of the helicopter rotor blades.

"I agree with you," Ernie said. "There's the processing plant."

As he got closer, he let off another burst of napolm at the wine tasting building, the wine processing area, and the oversized garage that stored five trucks and supplies. *Well, I guess I did my job, he thought.*

Ernie finally heard shots coming from the ground, so he veered off and headed back to Michael's place. He flew back to the hangar and landed safely.

"How did it go Ernie?" asked Manuel curiously. "I don't see any bullet holes anywhere. And that's always a good sign."

"Worked like a charm," Ernie said. "I almost picked up some bullet holes, but I got the job done."

Doug talked to the Paramount Guard Service manager and said, "We may have some trouble here today and maybe for the next few days. We *cannot* afford to lose *any* llamas or the wool that we've already sheared."

"We'll set ourselves up strategically, so that won't happen," said the leader of the group, as he pointed to various points on a map.

"How much longer before we get to San Ignacio?" Arturo asked.

"I estimate that our ETA should be about thirty minutes," said

Gaspar.

Gaspar called the airport tower asking for permission to land.

"This is the tower. You are not authorized to land at the San Ignacio Airport," said the air traffic controller.

"Why can't we land?" Gaspar shot back, bewildered.

"We have a reliable source," said the air traffic controller, "that you are carrying weapons and drugs on board your aircraft."

"This is ridiculous!" Gaspar said aloud.

"No, it's not," said Arturo snarling. "Find another airfield, fuel up and let's go back home. We'll go to Tel Aviv some other time." *It's Walter…..I just know it's him,* he thought. *He's meddling in all of this, and I know it.*

Lance called Rick and said, "We're ready for them."

"We're also on our way and should be touching down in a few hours," said Rick, and hung up.

Walter received a phone call from the Minister and said, "Thank you for warning us, Mr. Donleavy."

"It was my pleasure, Minister," Walter said. "By the way, how is the zebra wood trade doing these days?"

"It's working out just fine," said the Minister.

"I'm glad to hear that," Walter said. "Goodbye Minister."

Walter quickly called Rick and said, "I don't think you have to worry about your St. Augustine Ranch in San Ignacio."

"Why is that?" Rick asked, sounding baffled.

"I made a special call to my friend, the Minister of Velasco in Bolivia," Walter said. "If you remember, we gave him the shipping contract, for the zebra wood forest, when we bought the ranch in San Ignacio."

"Well, I'll be…," said Rick. "I'll call Doug and tell him that he can relax a little tonight."

"You may want to make sure he stays alert though," Walter said. "Just in case Leonard has some other tricks up his sleeve. He is not a stupid man."

"Thanks, Walter," Rick said, a little relieved. He quickly called Doug and relayed the message to him.

"Del, it looks like we're going back to pick up Ernie and his guys," Rick said, "and then fly back to Providence, Rhode Island.

"Duncan, we're flying to Rancagua, Chile," Walter said. "As soon as Rick lands, Aki, you and I are going to visit Mr. Souza."

"I'll be ready, Mr. Donleavy," Duncan said.

Walter asked. "Fred, any more information on Jason Segal?"

"There is, actually," Fred said, smiling at what he'd uncovered. "It's true that Jason came from Chile. However, he was born in Frankfurt, Germany. His mother passed away when he was young. However, his father is still alive and works at Deutsche Financial. His name happens to be… Rolf Freiburg. Although why he has, a different last name is a mystery. Does that ring any bells?"

"Yes it does," Walter said. *Another connection*, he thought. "My guess is that Leonard has been planning this whole charade for quite some time, possibly even while he was still working for me. I just don't get it! I have made him a multi-millionaire, many times over. He wouldn't have ever accumulated this kind of wealth had he been working as a CPA even for some of the larger firms!"

"Take it easy, Walter," Fred said, trying to calm him down.

"I can't take it easy!" Walter shouted and left the room.

Hilda, his housekeeper, heard all the commotion and went into Walter's study and said, "Mr. Donleavy, I know you are very unhappy about all of this. Can I offer you some tea and a slice of freshly made Bundt cake?"

He looked up, smiled at her and said, "That would be nice."

He watched Hilda walk out of his library. *I know what she's going through,* he thought, *because I've been through it many times myself.*

Chapter

29

Doug Arapahos lived almost all his whole life in Carrizozo, New Mexico. He did a two-year stint in the U.S. Army and stationed at Fort Huachuca, Arizona, which was close to the Mexican border and south of Tucson, Arizona. The Department of the Interior for Arizona ordered that a camp be established in the Huachuca Mountains. The fort had been the home of the 10th Cavalry "Buffalo Soldiers" for 20 years.

Doug had a unique MOS for a new soldier, and that was as an instructor for the new enlisted people. He didn't realize it at the time, but he had great teaching and listening skills.

"I think you're going to be just fine, son," said the Drill Sergeant. "Being an instructor in these times is going to keep you out of harm's way."

"Thanks, Sarge," Doug said. "I like teaching the recruits."

While he was stationed there, he took some psychology classes, and though he never got a degree, he felt he could now better understand how people functioned.

When he left the service, he held various odd jobs. Doug had an opportunity to work at a saddle shop in Carrizozo, New Mexico. He started working in the saddle shop, performing general cleanup and running errands. He loved the smell of leather as it was being worked.

"Is there a chance you could teach me how to make a saddle?" Doug asked, hopeful that he would say yes. .

"Are you kidding?" said the owner. "I didn't get to work on my first saddle for almost fifteen years. However, since you asked, maybe I can show you some of the tricks I use to make some of the more elaborate saddles."

"That would be great!" Doug said.

He stayed there for another two years. After all that time, he found out that he wanted to be a cowboy, working outdoors on the open range. What he finally realized was that the way movies portrayed a cowboy was not how it was in real life.

Doug was hired by Don Smith, who originally wanted him as the ranch manager for the San Lorenzo Ranch in Carrizozo, New Mexico. Horatio, who was the previous ranch manager, had originally moved to Bolivia from the ranch in Carrizozo, to manage the St. Augustine Ranch in San Ignacio, Bolivia. However, Horatio was killed in a shootout at the ranch in Bolivia and Don recommended Doug for the job. Doug moved to San Ignacio. Within a few short weeks and with some support from Frank Richter he had set up the operation and started shipping the llama wool to the *Balducci Couture* in Israel.

Chapter

30

Rick finally landed at the T. F. Green Airport in Warwick, Rhode Island. Walter was sitting in his car waiting until they taxied to their hangar and got out.

"I know this is short notice, but I need *you*, Ernie, to come with us," Walter said. "Aki, Duncan and I are going back to Rancagua, Chile. I need to settle this… for the last time. Rick I would rather have you back at my house to stay with Liz."

"But, Walter," Rick started to say.

"No *but's* about it," Walter said sternly. "Please, do as I ask this time….please," and he turned around and walked towards his plane.

Rick was a little put out as he watched everyone get in, taxi to the runway, and take off.

I sure wish I could go with them, he thought. *However, I also know that Walter has to see Leonard in person to get closure.*

They took off, and when they climbed to around thirty thousand feet, Walter came back to the cabin to meet with the other men in the group.

"I think it's safe to assume that by now Arturo, or Leonard as I've known him for over twenty-five years," Walter said, "knows that I've tried to stop him. As such, do not take any chances. A person like him, who probably still has a lot of money, will do anything and buy anything to achieve victory."

"I'm guessing that by now, he also knows we're coming for him," Ernie said. "And he'll probably be armed to the teeth."

"I agree," Walter said. "However, knowing how he thinks, may give us an advantage."

Duncan interrupted and said, "Mr. Donleavy, its Fred on the

phone."

"Yes, Fred, what is it?"

"It's just as you said Walter," Fred said. "Arturo turned around, stopped for fuel and is on his way back to the Santiago Airport in Rancagua, Chile."

"Okay, thanks, Fred," Walter said, happy that his plan worked.

"That was Fred confirming that Arturo is on his way back to Rancagua," Walter said. "Here is what I think we want to do," as Walter spent some time proposing a plan for after they landed.

"According to Michael, my friend that helped us before," Ernie said, "He has twelve-foot high chain link fencing with concertina wire and in some places is electrified. Over and above that, he probably has about thirty, plus, gun-toting security guards working for him."

"Maybe we don't have to storm the place," Aki said with authority. "That could be dangerous for us."

"What do you suggest, Aki?" Walter asked.

"Mr. Donleavy," Aki said, "he may, or may not know, that his vineyard and winery have been destroyed. Call him and boast a little. It will make him angry. I think that by then....he will be *very* angry. People make stupid mistakes when they are angry. To *me*, that means he will probably drive over to his vineyard, which is about a hundred miles away from his house. That will now make him very vulnerable."

"I like that idea," Walter said. "Go on."

"Also, while we track Arturo down," Aki said, "Ernie could destroy his compound. It's starting to get dark. If the explosion is big enough, he should be able to see it, even though he might be miles away. When he's seen it, he'll probably rush back to his compound."

"Then we'll wait for him and get him before he gets inside through either of his gates to his compound," Walter said.

"I think this will work," Aki said. "We just have to be a little patient."

"What do you think, Ernie?" Walter asked.

"I can do that," said Ernie smiling. "I'll call Michael, who helped us before. I'm sure he has some more napalm we can use. He can even make the call to Arturo since he actually works for him."

They had started their descent, when Ernie said, "This isn't the Santiago International Airport."

"Yes, I know that," Walter said. "I told Duncan to make up a flight plan to the Santiago International Airport. However, we're going make an emergency landing at Del Huenta Airport. I wouldn't want to let Arturo know we're coming."

"That's a good idea, Walter," Ernie said. *Always thinking*, he thought.

They landed and went directly to the field office and Duncan said, "We have engine trouble, and our mechanic is flying in to take care of our problem. Meanwhile, we'll be staying in town until he arrives."

"Thank you, senor," said the agent.

That went well, Walter thought.

Chapter

31

After Arturo had landed his plane at the airport, he drove directly to his compound. He sat and had a drink to relax his nerves.

"Gaspar! Have you found out if they landed yet?" Arturo asked loudly.

"They have not landed yet," Gaspar said. "Maybe they're not coming."

"Oh, they're coming all right," Arturo, said boldly. "He's coming for sure!"

The room was so still you could hear your heart beating. Suddenly the phone rang bringing Arturo out of his daze.

Arturo answered the phone and said, "What! What do you mean it's all gone! It can't be........it just can't be," as he slammed the phone down, with a shocked look on his face. "It's all gone.... the winery.....the vineyards....all gone up in smoke."

"Oh my God!" Gaspar said. "What do you want to do?"

"I've got to go there and see if anything is salvageable," Arturo said, frantically. Get some men, and let's get to my winery!"

They all piled into two cars and left by the front gate, where four guards are posted.

"Stay alert!" Arturo yelled out as he passed through the front gate.

They drove onto the main highway in caravan style.

"There they go," Walter said smiling mischievously. "Just as Aki had predicted."

"Ernie, this is Duncan. Arturo just left. I'd say give them about ten minutes, and then do what you do best. Good luck."

"Thanks, Duncan," Ernie said, as he took off in Michael's helicopter, fully loaded with napalm.

He again turned off the lights on the chopper so he wouldn't be spotted as he flew to Arturo's compound. He hovered for a moment over the property. Suddenly a barrage of napalm rockets hit the house, the swimming pool, the tennis courts and the twelve-car garage. The flames shot up so high they could be seen for miles.

Perfect shot, Ernie said to himself. *I think I'm getting to like this. Time to get back and land this thing.*

"What was that explosion?" Arturo asked in a panic. "Stop the car….stop the car!" The car came to a stop, and Arturo jumped out in a panic, looking in the direction of the explosion, and saw flames shoot hundreds of feet into the air. He stood there for a moment and thought to himself. *I think I know where those flames are coming from.*

"Where do you think that is coming from?" asked Gaspar.

"Where do *you* think, you idiot!" Arturo shouted out. "They lured us out here because now we're vulnerable! Let's get back to my house, quickly!"

"Well, Walter it looks like it worked," Ernie said.

"Yes, it did. Our very perceptive Aki knew," Walter said, smiling at Aki.

"I'm going to land in an open field just to the north of his compound," Ernie said. "I'm also going to the back gate of the compound, in case Arturo shows up and doubles back."

"Okay, but be careful," Walter said.

"Gaspar. Tell the men in the car behind us," Arturo yelling loudly, "to come in the other rear entrance gate and drive towards the front gate!"

"Got it," Gaspar said, as he relayed the message to the other car.

Soon the other car veered off to the service road that went to the back entrance gate.

Ernie saw the headlights of the second car approaching and was now about a hundred yards from the gate. Ernie came out of the bushes and walked up to the driver with guns drawn, and made him stop the car.

"Hi there. We haven't formally been introduced," Ernie said, holding a gun to his forehead and grabbing his jacket at the same time. "Now I have two options for you and your friends to consider. Option one is that you tell *all* your friends to step out of the car, put their guns on the ground, and then run like hell. This way they can live. On the other hand, option two is, that I just shoot all of you right *here*, right *now* and you *don't* get to run away to live."

"We will take the first option, senor," he said in a thick broken English voice.

Four men hastily got out of the car, dropped their guns, and ran down the road, in the direction they came from.

"Okay, now *you* can go. And don't look back," Ernie said, watching him also run in the same direction. *Well, that went well. I didn't even have to waste a bullet*, he thought.

Ernie hopped into the car, drove around the corner of the road, and slowly drove towards the other gate. The other guards quickly opened the gate to let Ernie drive in. Ernie got out of the car and made them the same offer. One of them didn't like the offer, so he went for his gun, and Ernie pistol-whipped him, and he went down.

"Would you like to take him with you?" Ernie asked.

They shook their heads, indicating "no" and ran in the same direction that the others had.

"Keep running and don't look back!" Ernie yelled and watched them disappear into the night.

Ernie got back into the car and drove past the house, which was still heavily engulfed in flames and towards the front gate. He jumped out and let the car keep rolling towards the front gate. The four guards, guarding the gate weren't prepared for this because they thought these were the other guards from the back of the property.

"Hold it!" Ernie yelled out and saw he caught them by surprise. "Drop your weapons…now! Hurry up! Unlock the gate and turn off the electricity for the gates and fences! Do you want to live to see another day?"

They looked at each other perplexed by the comment and just nodded their head.

"Then open these gates and run to the right or left of this road!" Ernie said, "And don't look back!"

Soon the lights from Arturo's car started to come closer to the front entrance, not realizing it was Ernie, who switched hats with one of the other men.

As Arturo was getting closer to his compound, he could see in the distance, with flames shooting five hundred feet high, that nothing was going to stop his place from burning to the ground. He drove up to the front of the gate, stopped the car, and just stared.

He was angry, and his clenched teeth showed it and said, "My place…..my home…it's all gone," Arturo, said.

As soon as he came to a stop, he was immediately surrounded by Aki, Duncan, and Ernie, who walked towards them with guns pointed directly at them.

"What's the meaning of this?" Arturo yelled loudly.

"Relax, Arturo, or should we call you…Leonard?" a voice called out from the bushes.

"Who are you and what are you doing here?" Arturo yelled loudly.

Walter came out from behind the bushes and out of the shadows.

Gaspar made a sudden move for his knives, and Duncan saw it. Just as quickly, he took a shot high, hoping to deter him. However, he still went after his knife. Ernie took careful aim and shot him in the head, right through the windshield. He slumped over the steering wheel.

"Why did you have to kill him?" Arturo shouted out.

"We need to talk," Walter said calmly, not answering him as he walked out into the lighted area. "You look a little different these days, Leonard, with your mustache and short-cropped gray hair, but the eyes....you can't change the eyes."

"You!" Arturo yelled out, seeing who it was, started to pull his gun from his shoulder holster.

"I wouldn't do that if I were you," Ernie said loudly, now standing out in the open.

"Haven't you done enough to kill my soul?" Arturo yelled out, as he quickly got out of his car.

As Arturo walked towards Walter, Ernie quickly rushed up to him and took his guns from him.

Chapter

32

Walter and Leonard walked towards the gate of his compound. A half-moon was shining, but the roaring fire lit up their way. The large lights mounted on top of the gate were now cracking and exploding from the heat that the fire was generating.

Walter said, "I seem to have said these words before Arturo… or Leonard……why? I didn't go to the funeral, but I agonized over you for weeks."

"Because there was still this hate inside of me that I just couldn't shake!" Leonard said proudly.

"How long have you been planning this?" Walter asked. "I even read in the newspapers that you died."

"I never actually died," Leonard, said grudgingly. "A very good friend of mine, Horst Heinzinger was named in my will, to inherit the house. He was instructed to sell it and do whatever he wanted with the money. The year before, I had already arranged to see a plastic surgeon in London, to change my facial features. After you left the last time we saw each other, I implemented my plan. I invited an individual who was about my same height and size to have a drink with me at my house. It was his last drink."

"Why carry on the deception?" Walter asked, still bewildered.

"Because I was unsuccessful the first time I tried to have you killed!" Leonard said loudly. "You and your precious Rick and Liz. You had everything……and I had nothing!"

Walter stood there and just shook his head in disbelief.

"I flew to Chile and purchased a vineyard with 500 acres of land," Leonard said. "The only good thing that came out of all of this is the vineyard and the winery. It was more successful than I could have imagined. There for a while I almost forgot about you, but then I suspect you had my vineyard destroyed."

"Yes I did," Walter said casually.

"Well, what started you up on this vendetta spree again?" Walter asked. "Surely I have done nothing to antagonize you again?"

"Remember when I was at your house the last time we met?" Leonard said. "I mentioned to you that with you breaking up your holdings, that you have extra office space in your building. You should try to sublease it to another company. I had already planned at the time to have my financial person's son from Frankfurt be in your building."

"I remember that and the individual," Walter said. "However, he didn't do anything that I could see."

"How do you think you got that virus on your system?" Leonard asked triumphantly.

"Are you saying that Jason Segal and Claus Livingston were in on this the whole time?" Walter asked.

"Jason knew about Claus because I told him to make sure he gets hired as the CFO of your company," Leonard said proudly. "Jason created a resume and left out that he worked for me at one time. Claus was actually very good and under different circumstances, could have possibly been my successor."

"But Leonard, I thought we worked all of that out?" Walter said.

"No! We actually never did!" Leonard said emphatically. "In your *own* mind, you may have thought it was worked out. I wanted to sit back and watch, so I could see how your precious company was going to go down in flames. However, I didn't have enough time and Claus panicked. That was one of the reasons he killed himself."

"All this you've been planning even before you left the company?" Walter asked loudly.

"Yes, I have!" Leonard said proudly. "I still remember when you came to visit me in Gstaad and tried to kill me with that brandy."

"That was purely out of preservation!" Walter said shouting louder and louder. "You know what I've been through during the war!"

"No! And I didn't care!" Leonard yelled out. "It's because of all those *rules* and the tight-fisted organization you created."

"It's *because* of those rules that we both made a lot of money,"

Walter shouted out. "You went to Yale and received a fantastic education. I, on the other hand, barely finished high school, and I was caught like a rat in a trap in the war. I had little, or no formal education and I used what I had to make it work. Granted, my ideas and plans may have been slightly unorthodox. But that's why I hired you!"

"I sometimes felt like the *token* employee!" Leonard said fiercely. "Doing all of your paperwork, because you didn't want to be visible at your company."

"I have never asked you to feel sorry for me," Walter said. "I put the war behind me. And oh yes, I *still* have reoccurring nightmares sometimes, but it never interfered with our relationship to build an empire that few people could even dream about."

"I still remember what I said to you as you knocked on the door," Leonard said. *"Isn't it a little late for visiting, Walter? I thought we said our goodbyes at your home.* "You said that you would like to leave this bottle of cognac for me as a final gesture of our friendship. I didn't really drink it. I later had it analyzed and found it had an Asian type of poison in it. It would create a heart attack type of death."

"I guess for that.....I'm sorry," Walter said sarcastically.

"You said you reviewed all the documents I created for you, Rick and Liz," Leonard said. "Well, I also made a duplicate copy of all of those documents and put my name back on them."

"My son and wife died because of you!" Leonard said.

"But again Leonard, your son did this to himself!" Walter shouted back. "Don't you remember the problems it caused us with all of those other investors? If it were not for me, Victor Chen would have killed Peter in a most gruesome way. I spent millions buying his freedom, even though Peter almost ruined *me*. All so he could play the role of a millionaire entrepreneur."

"It could have been handled differently!" Leonard shouted, trying to stay calm.

Ernie and Duncan stood there, with guns drawn, concerned for Walter's safety because they were now shouting louder and louder.

"No, it could not!" Walter said loudly. "Your son had an opportunity few people would *ever* get in life. He chose to squander it by trying to play being a big shot! He died because *you* did not teach him the basics of life as it relates to the business world!"

"That's not true!" Leonard fired back.

"You're obviously in denial," Walter commented.

"The day is not over yet, my friend," Leonard said menacingly.

"You killed my friend, Jacob," Walter said. "For that, I cannot forgive, *or* forget."

"That case of wine was meant for you!" Arturo said still shouting.

"I know it," Walter said. Suddenly two shots rang out. One to Arturo's chest, and the other to his head. Walter watched as Leonard slowly fell to the ground, with a shocked look on his face.

"Goodbye, my friend.....again," Walter said quietly, turned and walked back towards the van.

Ernie and Duncan heard the shots, came running up to Walter and saw Leonard laying on the ground with blood flowing from his head and chest.

"Let's put him inside his gate," Walter said. "I'll make an anonymous call to the local police that he was shot and that his real name is Leonard Schultz. I'll suggest that they bury him in his family crypt in Palmyra Cemetery." *Now he will be buried and use the place that he had moved eight thousand miles away*, he thought.

"Are you all right, Walter?" Ernie asked.

Walter said, "Yes, I'm fine. However, I've fired this gun twice since you gave it to me. I need a new one about the same size because I'm never going to fire this one again. I'm going to retire it in my vault because now it has sentimental value to me. I lost two very close friends this week."

"I'll take care of it, Walter," Ernie said.

"Let's go home, boys," Walter said solemnly. "I think we've done enough damage for this week."

"Yeah I agree," Ernie said.

"You boys are all welcome to stay at my house to rest up before you go home," Walter said.

Chapter

33

It was now almost noon the next day. Rick and Liz were waiting for Walter at his house, by the front door. Walter got out of the car and walked up the familiar steps thinking. *Just last week, Jacob walked by, and I asked him to get rid of a case of wine.*

"Would you mind if we talked a little later?" Walter asked. "It's been a trying several days, and I'm exhausted."

Rick and Liz watched Walter walk up the stairs, noticing he didn't have that normal *bounce* when he walked.

"We'll wait for him," Rick said. "I'm sure he's going to be all right."

Walter walked upstairs, directly to his bedroom, took his clothes off, and took a shower. *It feels good to wash off the filth I just went through*, he thought. Suddenly and for no apparent reason, he was taken back to when he washed up when he was in the concentration camp, and Jacob was his friend. *Why did it have to be him*, he thought. He got out of the shower, dressed, and went back downstairs to sit with Rick and Liz. As he walked downstairs, he reminisced as he looked down into the living room and his library that he uses as his office. *I remember when I had that oak paneling brought over from the Black Forest in Germany*, he thought. *What's the use thinking about it…it won't bring Jacob back no matter how much I wished it.*

"Hi, Uncle Walter." Liz walked up to him, hugged him and saw the sadness in his eyes. "Are you all right?"

"No, I'm *not* all right," Walter, said. "However, life must go on. I'm just so glad that you two are doing well. I think we should toast to a new tomorrow." He went to his liquor cabinet, where he kept his special blue cut crystal. He stood there, because every time he got one or more of his glasses, he also remembered when and where he purchased them. *That was a long time ago*, he thought. "I'm sorry. I'm just not myself right now."

"That's okay Walter," Rick said. "You've been through an awful lot these past few weeks. What can I do to help you through this?"

"Nothing for now, but thank you for the offer," Walter said. "I just have to deal with it."

"Why don't you come out to the ranch for a little while," Liz suggested. "It would do you a world of good....I'm sure."

"We'll see," Walter said. "We'll see. Right now, I have to go and hire a new CFO for my company. If I'm not careful, I'll be broke."

"Just a suggestion, Walter," Rick said. "But, do you think that Frank Richter, my CFO, could help you for a little while?"

"I'll think about that," Walter said. "For the time being, let's just enjoy the moment."

About that time, Hilda popped in and asked, "Would anyone like some tea or coffee?"

"I think we could all go with a spot of tea, don't you think?" Walter said. "However, I would very much appreciate it if you would join us, Hilda."

Chapter

34

Before Walter flew to Frankfurt, he had Fred access Leonard's bank account and told him to transfer twenty million dollars to his personal bank account in the Cayman Islands.

"I'll tell you what to do with it when I get back to the house," Walter said. *Leonard's not going to miss the money, and Rolf will probably take what's left anyway,* he thought.

That same day, in the morning, Duncan flew Walter and Frank Richter to Frankfurt, Germany, to meet with Rolf Freiberg.

"I brought you with me, to finish this mess that Leonard had created," Walter said. "I talked to Rick, or rather he talked to me about having you spend some time at my headquarters office and get an inside look at how I operate."

"I am just thrilled that you're giving me this opportunity," Frank said enthusiastically.

"You have no idea what you have just signed on for," Walter said.

They drove up to a very large and ornate building, built in the late 1800's that seemed to have missed being bombed during the war.

They walked up the sumptuous cement steps and past the enormous gargoyles standing on each side of the glass and polished doors. They went directly to an information booth.

"Would you tell Mr. Freiburg that Walter Donleavy is here to clear up the estate of Arturo Souza and Leonard Schultz?"

Walter and Frank were directed to Rolf's office. He was a little startled seeing Walter.

"What can I do for you, Mr. Donleavy?" asked Rolf sarcastically.

"I assume that by now you've heard that Arturo Souza or Leonard Schultz is dead."

"No, I had not," Rolf, answered back.

"I'm going to give you five dollars, and you're going to sign over the Santa Rita Ranch in Maipo Valley, Chile to me.

"Why would I do that?" Rolf asked arrogantly.

Walter very casually said, "If word got out what you did during the war, it would not go well for you. You see, I also have many influential friends with the German Government. I know what you did *during* the war, and you were lucky you were able to disappear. I hope we understand each other, Mr. Freiburg,"

Rolf was fidgeting in his chair and staring at Walter. He knew he had to do something, so he reluctantly went to his cabinet and pulled out the file for the *Santa Rita Ranch* in Maipo Valley, Chile.

"I also checked, and I know you have power of attorney for all of his assets," Walter said. "Do with them what you wish. I just want the ranch."

Hearing that news, Rolf quickly signed all the papers and gave them to Walter.

"Thanks," Walter said, "and here is your five dollars for the grant deed. I know it is customary to give you a check, but I'm sure you're going to take Arturo's money anyway, so I don't think a check is necessary."

"Quite right Mr. Donleavy," said Rolf. "It isn't necessary.

"Oh, one last thing, your son Jason Segal is flying back to Frankfurt as we speak. All of his equipment now belongs to me. I could have sent him back to you in pieces, but I was kind."

"Thank you, Mr. Donleavy," Rolf said, now perspiring profusely.

"Goodbye and I hope never to *hear* or *see* you again," Walter said, and got up and left his office.

"Goodbye Mr. Donleavy," said Rolf, turning chalk white from the conversation he just had.

As they left the building and walked towards the car where Duncan was waiting, Frank said, "Mr. Donleavy that was amazing!"

"No it wasn't," Walter said. "I just blackmailed an individual for a piece of property that cost me five dollars. This is what I do and I'm very good at it. Never forget this lesson. Information is the key to success, but you have to know what to do with this data in order to be successful."

"Rick, we're flying back from Germany," Walter said. "The Santa Rita Ranch in Maipo Valley, Chile, now belongs to you. We'll see you in a day or two, so we can talk a little more about your new llama ranch and Frank's future."

How did he accomplish that? Rick wondered. *After everything that has happened, he's still negotiating for new business.*

Chapter

35

Victor Chen was told by Walter who is a business associate, of a casino and resort in Paris, which was closed down by the gaming commission for gaming violations and tax evasion. He contacted the Mayor of Paris, Pascal Renaud, and inquired about purchasing the resort. What originally attracted him was its location – across the street, and in the shadows of the Eiffel Tower.

Victor and his son, Quan flew to Paris from Macau late one night in his private plane.

"This could be very lucrative for the family," Victor said happily.

"It also sounds like it will be a lot of work to get it reopened," Quan said.

"Yes, it will, my son," Victor said. "However, I have created a plan that is broken down into three phases. In the first phase, after we receive our license from the French Gaming Commission, is to get the casino up and running and close down the hotel temporarily in order to start the renovations. The casino will be generating income for us, and that money will be used to start phase two of the renovation, of the first half of the hotel. When that is complete, people will stay at the hotel, and we use those profits to start phase three of the restoration process to the other half of the hotel."

"It still sounds like a long-time process," Quan said.

"I think we can do this in about twenty-four months," Victor said. "In this way, our personal cash outlay will be greatly reduced, and we can use the profits to pay for most of the renovations. This will also reduce our tax liability tremendously for at least four years."

"I must warn you, Mr. Chen, that the *Paradisio Casino and Resort* is going to be difficult to acquire," said Pascal. "There is also another company looking at it for the same reasons. In either case, you will still have several other problems."

"What problems are those, Mr. Renaud?" asked Victor politely and eager for any information.

"The previous owner, who is out on bail, is awaiting trial for tax evasion by INTERPOL as well as agents for the New York and London Stock Exchange," Pascal said. "The whole thing is a mess and in the court's hands starting in Stockholm, Sweden. While he is awaiting trial, they all felt that keeping Franco in Sweden and away from Paris, was a good thing. It could be years away from being settled."

"Does he have any family I could talk to?" asked Victor.

"None that we're aware of," said Pascal.

"What is the owner's name?" Victor asked.

"His name is Franco DeMarco," Pascal said. "Even though he's out on bail, he has to stay in Stockholm, Sweden under some type of house arrest."

"What if I could convince him to sell me his interest in the place," Victor asked politely. "I would then pay any back taxes still owed as well as whatever the *Pari Mutuel Urbain*, which is the French Gaming Commission fines are. Would that work?"

"Yes. I think that would work, Mr. Chen," said Pascal sounding more positive.

"After that, we should be receiving the gaming license? Victor asked.

"Yes, I think that can be arranged," said Pascal.

Victor and his son, Quan Chen, flew to Stockholm, Sweden two days later, to meet with Franco DeMarco, to negotiate a deal to purchase his interests in the *Paradisio Casino and Resort* in Paris, France. Victor brought his son, Quan, so he could see firsthand how to negotiate a more complex purchase. They drove to his house where he was under house arrest.

"Mr. Franco, my name is Victor Chen, and this is my son, Quan."

"You're the person that contacted me several days ago,"

said Franco. "Come in. Although I've already been told that I shouldn't sell my place."

"Thank you for your hospitality," Victor said as he bowed to him.

"I'll come right to the point," Victor, said not listening to Franco's comment. "We have a very generous offer to buy out your interest in the casino and resort, which you own in Paris, France."

"Who are you? And who told you that my casino was for sale?" Marco spoke out loudly.

"In this type of business word gets around," said Victor smiling. "I already own several successful casinos myself."

"What makes you think you can come here and try to buy my place!" Franco demanded angrily.

"Let me enlighten you a little bit," Victor said, trying to be pleasant sounding. "Your various bank accounts have been frozen due to tax evasion. The back taxes and penalties will take a big part of that. Your creditors will probably take some of that also. What you may have left will probably be taken by your lawyers. The only thing you have left that has not been frozen...is your casino, but only because it is already closed down. Evidently, the French Gaming Commission and INTERPOL felt that all the bank accounts you have will cover any penalties and fines you will have to pay."

"How do you know all that?" Franco demanded again, infuriated with the prospect of losing his casino. "I still have some influence in France!"

"Mr. DeMarco....you're kidding yourself," Victor said, trying to sound humble.

"I don't know...I'll think about it," Franco said, unhappy with the conversation so far.

"There is also the *Pari Mutuel Urbain* which is the French Gaming Commission," Victor continued. "I understand they are also waiting in line for the fines you owe them. In the end, they will also revoke any licenses you may have existing, and you'll never be granted another license on *any* continent. In other words, by the time that your trial comes up, and potential incarceration time, along with your lawyer's fees, you'll be dead broke. The value of your casino is going down, every day that it sits vacant.

Because it sits unoccupied, you could be vandalized, and then it will be worth even less. "

"Well, you've made it very clear that I have no options!" Franco said angrily. "It sounds like you have worked all of this out already!"

"Yes, I have. One other thing, Mr. DeMarco. Any money I give you would be yours," Victor quickly said. "I could put this into an escrow account, and you can have it available to you anytime you like. We could set up a special account that only your friend Herbert would know. This way he could hold it for you. Your second wife has filed for divorce, so give her the house and that part is over."

"How do you know about Herbert?" Franco yelled out, as he stood up.

"It seems he has not been very quiet about your relationship with him," Victor said. "I'm sure that by now your wife obviously knows because it was in the newspapers; however, I'm not here to judge. I'm trying to offer you some closure to this problem you currently have."

Franco was thinking about the offer. *I have worked almost my whole life to have this casino,* he thought. *Now it's potentially gone.*

"Think about it, Mr. DeMarco," Victor said as he stood up. "We will be staying at the Continental Hotel for two days. Call me and tell me what you've decided," and Victor handed him a business card with a phone number on it.

Victor Chen had many years of experience building as well in managing the casino and hotel business. He currently owns three in Macau, one in Johannesburg, South Africa and he built two casinos in Montana for the Chief of the Crow Nation, Chief Running Buffalo.

As they drove back to their hotel, Victor called Walter and said, "Mr. Donleavy, I want to thank you for the information about the *Paradisio Casino and Resort* in Paris, France. I'm investigating this and I think it might be worthwhile."

"You're very welcome, Mr. Chen," Walter said. "I received the information from a third party, so I'm not sure how reliable the information is. On the surface, it's at least advisable to look at the property. Good luck on your new venture."

As Walter hung, he had thought about purchasing the hotel for himself and moving to Paris full time. However, in light of the problems he had with Apollo and then finding out it was Leonard, who tried to have him killed, it lost its luster.

Chapter

36

Franco DeMarco, whose given name was Kacpar Naftali grew up on the streets of Krakow, Poland. His parents and brother were killed during World War II in separate air raids. He survived only by stealing whatever food he could get, and killed anybody who prevented him from staying alive. He was one of the few that was able to find his way to Northern Italy. He hid out with some of the local peasants who owned a farm in a remote part of the country.

He worked on the small plot of land the farmer had. That helped him understand what his parents went through, as they worked their farm. He stayed with the farmer for over three years, and they treated him as if he were their own son. However, he was yearning for a better life and often dreamed of being rich. Unfortunately, he had no idea how to become rich, and since he lacked a real education, he traveled around, until he was bored and then moved on.

He finally ended up in Venice, walking around the main streets of the town, and through the finer shopping centers. He stopped in front of one store and looked in through the large picture window and thought, *I wish I could have a pair of shoes or a sports coat like that.*

As he stood there, a young woman walked up to him and said, "Those are very nice clothes, aren't they?"

"Yes, very nice," he said smiling, as he turned to her. "Unfortunately, I'm about fifty dollars short," trying to make light of the situation.

"My name is Madeline DeMarco. That's my father's store, you were admiring. What is your name?"

He hesitated and remembered a designer's name on some shirts he saw that morning and said, "Franco."

"My father wants to expand his store," she said. "However, the only way he can thrive in this cutthroat business is to do something different. You have that slim physique that would look good in our clothes."

"Thank you. But what would this entail?" Franco asked being curious.

"We would have you wear different clothes every few days," she said. "We would also have our window displays show that same ensemble."

Franco thought it was a great idea because each day he would wear different clothes and model them as he walked throughout the store. He would wear a special suit, tie, shirt, slacks, and shoes. He walked around inside, then stood in front, looking into the main picture window displaying a mannequin wearing the same outfit. Sales increased immediately, and within six months, Madeline took over the store and started dating Franco at the same time.

Two years later, they were married. At that time, Franco decided to use Madeline's last name, because of the store's name – DeMarco sounded so regal. They stayed married for another three years until he was caught with another woman, in their bed.

"How could you!" she screamed.

"It was easy," he said. "You don't attract me anymore."

She ended up divorcing him, but not before, she gave him enough money to leave her alone. She also had a very close friend, Bella, from Apollo Enterprises, who helped make sure he wouldn't be back to bother her.

From there, Franco just drifted and ended up in Paris working in a small casino. The owners saw how good he was at taking care of deadbeats who didn't pay off their gambling debts. They offered him a job as head of security for their casino. He was now dressing well and cracking heads at the same time. Soon, he had a staff that did the dirty work for him. As time went on, he grew to several different key roles in the organization.

The casino crowd started growing as they added more hotel rooms and enlarged the casino area at the same time. At some point, they made Franco a partner. As time went on, the other partners died or mysteriously disappeared until only Franco was left.

After Victor left, Franco called his business lawyer and told him about the offer. "That's what he's offering. What do you think?"

"I think if he's offering that," said his lawyer arrogantly, "then he may pay a little more. He's obviously a successful casino and hotel operator and knows the value of your property."

"Okay, and thanks," Franco said, now more confused than ever.

Franco spent the next several hours considering Victor's offer. The more he thought about it, the more he didn't want to sell. *I still have friends that can manage the casino for me*, he thought. *However, do I trust them enough not to skim money from me? Then there are the licenses and his back taxes.*

"Quan, you have just seen how we negotiate when we want something that will benefit the *family*," said Victor.

"But father, if we pay all the fines and back taxes," Quan said, "it will cost more than the place is worth."

"My son, you listen, but you do not hear anything," Victor said. "When we were still in Paris, I had previously negotiated a deal with the mayor to pay only twenty percent of the fines and back taxes. This also includes the various licenses required to have a full casino and hotel operating. After all, the city will benefit much more when the casino opens again."

"That sounds great so far," said Quan. "But..."

"Let me finish," Victor said, smiling. "I also think that when we open an account for Franco, whether it's in Mr. DeMarco's or Herbert's name, someone will find out and freeze the account. They will probably also take their share from that if they want. In other words, we have still bought a casino and hotel in the middle of Paris for a great price."

Victor Chen was the oldest of five sons of the Xingang families that are located in the Nanchang Provence of China. Just before the Chinese Civil War broke out, which lasted ten years, the surviving members of the Xingang family had smuggled gold bars and jewels out of China and into Sapporo, Japan. They stayed in relative hiding until the war was over. The father, mother, two daughters, and five sons made up the family. The father and mother died before they could go back to their homeland and restart their life. However, the seven surviving children created a powerhouse organization called – *The Li Chan Group*.

Once the war was over, the family tried to go back to their home. The war partially destroyed the family home, but the land was still there. However, because it was considered *spoils of war*, General Xingcho confiscated it as his own. The Xingang family asked if they could buy it back, but he just laughed and refused. Within two days, they had a signed bill of sale from the General for the property, and the General was never seen again.

The family developed a reputation in the region for helping other farmers with similar problems. Their fee for this *help* was nominal because they wanted them as friends and long-term allies. Soon they had developed strategic relationships with many of the more prosperous families. They finally had enough money to open a nightclub they called *The Washington*. *The Washington* was chosen because they wanted to attract U.S. visitors who had more money to spend. It served as a hotel and casino. Within five years, they opened two other hotels and casinos in Macau.

They grew into eight families –all part of the *Li Chan Group*. They kept a low profile and slowly started buying surrounding land and property for future projects.

Chapter

37

Franco paced in his living room like a caged animal, wondering what he should do. He finally decided to call Victor back and ask him to sweeten the deal.

"Mr. Chen," Franco said. "My financial advisor said your offer is not enough."

"I see," Victor said and paused. "I'm not sure I can pay more for your place. Remember, I still have to refurbish almost everything. However, let me call you back," and hung up the phone.

"Father…" Quan started to say.

"Please wait a moment my son," Victor held up his hand and gave him the, *be quiet* sign and counted to fifteen.

Victor called Franco back and said, "I have talked to my other partners in Macau. They feel that we have made a fair offer. If that is your final word, then I must regretfully pass on this deal. Thank you for your time," and hung up the phone.

"Father…" Quan again started to say.

"Please wait a moment, my son," Victor said, again holding up his hand.

Ten minutes passed, and the phone rang.

"Hello?" Victor asked.

"This is Franco. I just talked to my financial advisors again, and…they have come around, reluctantly, and I've agreed to your numbers."

"That is wonderful news," Victor said, winking at his son and smiling. "I'll have all the papers drawn up today. I will also bring a Notary Public to notarize the documents."

Franco immediately called Herbert and said, "Herbert, now

listen to me carefully."

"Oh, I'm so happy you called Franco," Herbert said cheerfully.

"Yeah, and I miss you too," Franco said hastily. "Go to a new bank and open a new account in *your* name only. Put about five hundred dollars into it. When you're done, call me with the bank name and the account number. Got it?"

"Okay I can do that," Herbert said. "When am I going to see you again?"

"Soon, I hope,' Franco said. "Now do as I told you," feeling a little euphoric as he hung up the phone.

Listening on a tapped line was Ludvig Eriksson, the INTERPOL agent who originally found out about the secret bank accounts.

"This is fantastic!" Ludvig yelled out. "Did you hear that? Another potential account we can access as soon as he opens the account and money transfers into it. This way we can make sure we collect *all* of the back taxes and penalties."

"That was a great idea of yours to let him stay as house arrest rather than in jail," Sir David said ecstatically.

"It looks that way," said Ludvig, who was also involved in the original capture of Franco DeMarco.

The next afternoon Victor and Quan went back to Franco's house, with a Notary Public, and signed all the papers.

"Thank you, Mr. DeMarco," Victor said and bowed to him. "We will make the transfer of funds, to your bank as soon as the bank opens tomorrow."

"You've got yourself a great place, Mr. Chen," Franco said, feeling he'd bested him.

"We'll see," Victor said. "I still have a lot of work to do, Mr. DeMarco, before I can open the place for tourists."

"Goodbye and good luck," Franco said glumly, still wondering if he did the right thing.

"Good luck, yourself," said Victor, who bowed and left with his son and the Notary Public.

Epilogue

Ernie went to Walter's headquarters building, the next day and found Jason Segal working in his office.

"Mr. Donleavy would like you to leave this building and never come back," Ernie said informally as he sat down on his couch.

"I have a lease that will hold up in any court," Jason said arrogantly.

"While that might be so," Ernie said, "you'll never exercise that court date....especially if you're dead. I suggest you take whatever you want right now and leave. A gentleman is standing by the elevator with a ticket to fly you back to Frankfurt so you can see your father."

"You can't threaten me!" Jason said. "I have rights!"

"Did I fail to mention that I can also ship you to Frankfurt in pieces and in a box?" Ernie said casually.

Jason cringed a little.

"Your *father*, Rolf Freiberg, is being visited by Mr. Donleavy as we speak," Ernie mentioned to him.

Jason now had a worried look on his face, and immediately got up, grabbed his coat and briefcase, and headed towards the elevator. He passed Fred as he went down in the elevator.

"Fred, you can come in here now," Ernie said. "Your turn to do what you do best."

Fred went into the small computer room that had the mainframe computer, turned everything off, and then used an electromagnet to wipe out any data residing on any part of the servers.

Ernie was true to his word and took Michael, Thomas, and Pete to the Red Dragon in Macau. As he walked in the front door, he was met by Victor Chen.

"How are you, Mr. Slater," Victor said, shaking his hand.

"I brought with me several of my friends to show them a little excitement," Ernie said. "Are my two girlfriends here tonight?"

"Of course. They are waiting in your suite," Victor said.

"Thank you, Mr. Chen. My friends may also want to be introduced to some of your girls."

"That can all be arranged," Victor said as he bowed to his guests.

"One word of caution, fellas," Ernie said, turning to his friends. "Mr. Chen is a great person, so don't piss him off and embarrass me in the process."

The following week, Walter called Steve, Fred, and Ernie on a conference call from his home and said, "Firstly I want to thank you all for the support you've given me these last few weeks. As a result, I'm transferring to each of you, two million dollars. It's just my way of saying.......thank you. Ernie I'm giving you an additional two hundred thousand to pay for the napalm you used from your friend Michael."

"Wow, we didn't expect that," they said almost in unison.

"I told you all a long time ago that each of you I consider one of my children," Walter said. "I also value your loyalty, which to me is....priceless."

"Thank you, Walter," they all said

"Nevertheless, it's yours, to grow your business or do whatever you wish," Walter said. Rick has a new ranch in Chile to support the growth that Mustafa has projected. Good night, fellas."

Walter sat back in his chair, taking in all that has happened in the last several weeks and was content with the outcome.

Walter opened his vault located in his library behind the oak paneling. He opened the second safe inside the larger vault. He took out his Derringer Cobra pistol, which he used to kill Leonard Schultz, and carefully put it into one of his red felt-lined drawers.

This is how I will finally remember you, my friend, he thought. *Every time I open this drawer and see this gun, I will remember that you killed Jacob.*

He closed the door to his inner safe and then the larger vault door. He closed the door to his study, walked over, sat in his chair, and waited for the sun to go down. As he looked out of his large windows, he saw that the black and the white swans were swimming in his small lake, with not a care in the world.

Del finally called Gail and said, "I'm on my way back to Fort Collins. Are you available this week to fly out?"

"I think I can swing that," Gail said enthusiastically. "Tomorrow is Friday. How about if I fly out in the morning?"

"Great!" Del said. "I'll pick you up at the airport, and we'll go from there."

Characters – Retribution (the year is 1998)

1. **Dr. Rick Benedict (In 1998 Rick is 48 years old)**
   a. born Jan 29, 1950, as Richard Teaubel
   b. (1955) Came to America when he was (5 yrs. old)
   c. Rick and Liz got married on June 11, 1987
   d. Llama and alpaca ranches –
       i. San Lorenzo Ranch in Carrizozo, New Mexico
       ii. St. Augustine Ranch in San Ignacio, Bolivia.
       iii. Santa Rita Ranch in Maipo Valley, Chile
   e. Monarch Ranch Meat Processing Plants
       i. Billings, Montana
       ii. Fort Collins, Colorado
2. **Dr. Elizabeth (Liz) Hildebrand. (In 1998 Liz is 47 years old)**
   a. born Mar 15, 1951, as Elizabeth Bowan
   b. Liz married Bryan in 1977 and changed her name to Hildebrand
   c. Rick and Liz got married on June 11, 1987, changed the name to Benedict
   d. Now manages the Three Forks Restaurant and Lodge in four states. Also the Wagon Wheel restaurant in Fort Collins, Colorado
   i. Jennifer Billingsly – Liz's new CFO located in Fort Collins to take care of her new companies.
3. **Walter Donleavy/Alfred Berger (in 1998 Walter is 73)**
   a. Uncle to Rick and Liz, entrepreneur, major businessperson, has deep secrets. Victor Magionetta (the name he used in Paris)
   b. Born on February 27, 1925, in London England
   c. At age, 15 went to school in Florence to learn oil painting techniques.
   d. Age 18 was rounded up by the Nazis and sent to Sachsenhausen concentration camp just outside Berlin, Germany was there for two years.
   e. No info about Walter/Alfred before 1954
   f. Name of his company is **Monarch Enterprises**.
4. **Leonard Schultz/Arturo Souza** – Chief lawyer and business

negotiator for Walter Donleavy. Graduated from Yale in 1960. His wife's name is Cynthia. Was the COO of Walter's business holdings, **Monarch Enterprises**. Born in 1938, he is now 60. He moved the family crypt to the Palmyra Cemetery in Rancagua, Chile

    a. Peter Schultz – Leonard's' son who started working with his father after graduating from the USC Marshall School of Business and the Leventhal School of Accounting.

    b. Cynthia is his wife, who died in Gstaad, Switzerland in a sanitarium.

5. **Stephen Weisen** – Started his own security firm called Weisen Security. He was also the captain of Liz's yacht at one time.

    a. born 1949

    b. (1957 Came to America when he was (5 yrs. old)

    c. (1977-1979) Army Ranger

    d. Created the Weisen Security Company for the US and Romanesque Security Company for all of Europe, Asia, and Africa.

6. **James Kingston** – Vice President Special security to assist Steve with any problems. Manages the Rome operations for Weisen Security.

7. **Pete Lindquist** – works for Steve as part of new Weisen Security

8. **Thomas Harrington** - works for Steve as part of new Weisen Security.

9. **Dorothy (Waylon) Weisen** – sister of Jimmy Hackensack and now Steve's wife.

10. **Duncan Houston** - Walter's pilot and Security detail. His given name was actually Hakarson, but the family changed it because of it too difficult to pronounce

    a. Hannah Houston – Sister to Duncan and an assistant district attorney for Los Angeles.

    b. Conrad and Martha Houston – Parents of Duncan and Hannah. Came from Sweden in the late 60s.

11. **Jacob Teaubel/Fredrick & Geraldine Leiter** – Gatekeeper of Walter Donleavy estate (Rick's actual parent)

    a. Came over to the United States in 1960

    b. Died in 1998

    c. Married **Hilda Lowenstein** in 1997.

12. **Hilda Lowenstein/Anna & Christopher Bowens** –
    Housekeeper to Walter Donleavy estate (Liz's actual parent)
        a. Came over to the United States in 1959
        b. Married **Jacob Teaubel** in 1997

13. **Fred Tremane** – was Corporal/Master Sergeant in the Army
    and became a Forensic accountant.
        a. Evan Singleton – works for Fred as a new associate.
        b. Martha Honeycutt – works for Fred as a new associate.

14. **Arturo Souza** – actually is Leonard Schultz. He had plastic
    surgery done to his face.
        a. He owns Adolpho Vincenti Vineyards, in Portio, Chile.
        b. He also purchased the Santa Rita Ranch in Maipo
        Valley of Chile.

15. **Gaspar Marceau** – is **Arturo Souza** pilot. He was a fighter
    pilot for the French Air Force

16. **Milton de La Cross** –
        a. He was originally the head chef and General Manager
        at *The Alpinhoff Restaurant* in Providence, Rhode Island.
        b. Now head chef and General Manager of *The Blue
        Lobster* – located in Mystic, Maine.

17. **Danielle Smith** – was the part-time girlfriend of Fred
    Tremane, and married her in 1997. She is also the brother of
    Don Smith.

18. **Claus Livingston** – Walters new CFO for Monarch
    Enterprise

19. **Don Smith** – Rick's ranch Forman at the Monarch Ranch.
        a. Maureen Smith – Don's wife

20. **Ernie Slater** – A CIA friend who taught Rick some simple
    burglary techniques. Is now part of Walter's special team.
        a. Wilber Watkins – works in Ernie' office as an assistant.

21. **Aki Watanabe and his wife Tomichi** – beef wrangler of
    Walter's Kobe beef ranch in Rhode Island. In his prior life
    was a professional Samurai bodyguard for one of the oldest
    and wealthiest families in Hong Kong.

22. **Frank Richter** – Rick's CFO for the businesses he managed,
    primarily the Monarch Ranch and the two alpaca and llama
    ranches. Also the son of Paul Mathews, the famous European

cat burglar. He went to Yale to receive his degree.

    a. Johanna Mitlander – Frank's new girlfriend he met several months ago.

23. **Victor Chen** is Head of the Li Chan Group. He and Walter have made various deals together. His casinos

    a. Macau, China

        i. The Washington Resort and Casino in province of China

        ii. The Red Dragon Casino and Resort in Macau

        iii. The Blue Grotto Casino and Resort in Macau

    b. Johannesburg, South Africa –

        i. The Golden Reef Casino and Resort.

    c. Paris, France

        i. The Champs-Élysées, casino, and Resort

24. **Quan Chen** – Victor Chen's older son. Went to school at USC in California

25. **Pascal Renaud** – Mayor of Paris that Victor Chen contacted to purchase the now-closed *Paradisio Casino and Resort*.

26. **Del Babinski** – Rick's new pilot for the plane Walter sold him for a dollar.

27. **Gail Singleton** – Del's girlfriend living currently in Florida

28. **Mustafa Shamir** - He became the CEO of Balducci Couture located in Tel Aviv, Israel.

29. **Horst Heinzinger** – close friend to Leonard Schultz and helped him disappear from Gstaad.

30. **Rolf Freiburg** – Worked for Deutsche Financial, as the banker for Leonard in Frankfurt, Germany. Helped him buy Adolpho Vincenti Vineyards, in Portio, Chile and Santa Rita Ranch in Maipo Valley of Chile.

31. **Jason Segal** – rented space in Walter's building in Providence, Rhode Island. His business is as an electronics entrepreneur. He is the son of Rolf Freiburg.

32. **Juan Cristobal** – previous owner of the Adolpho Vincenti Vineyards, in Portio, Chile

33. **Franco Demarco** –His Casino was called the *Paradisio Casino and Resort*. He is in Stockholm, Sweden awaiting trial on tax evasion charges. His actual given name is Kacpar, Naftali,

34. **Detective Mark Shannon** – Detective for the Providence

police department.

35. **William Devonshire** – former owner of the Santa Rita Ranch in Maipo Valley in Chile

36. **Bryon Worthington** – the Chief of Police for Providence, Rhode Island, and friend to Walter.

37. **Vilosco** - bartender at the Mr. Belvedere Restaurant in Portio.

38. **Doug Arapahos** – The new ranch manager for the San Lorenzo Ranch in Carrizozo, New Mexico after Horatio moved to Bolivia.

39. **Michael** - helped Ernie when he was in Chile with a helicopter and some napalm.

40. **Lance Driscoll** – the ranch Forman of the St Augustine Ranch in San Ignacio, after Horatio was killed in a shoot-out at that ranch.

41. **Harry Palmer** – Agent for the New York Stock Exchange,

42. **Sir David Hayworth** – Agent for the London Stock Exchange

43. **Ludvig Eriksson** – Agent for INTERPOL, based in Lisbon

44. **Walter's three restaurants**
   a. The Matterhorn – located in Manhattan, New York
   b. The Alpinhoff – located in Providence, Rhode Island
   c. The Blue Lobster – located in Mystic, Maine

45. **Liz's restaurants**
   a. (12) The Three Forks Restaurant and Lodge – located in four states.
   b. Restaurant Locations for Three Forks Restaurant and Lodge
      i. Montana **(5)** Billings, Butte, Bozeman, Missoula, Great Falls,
      ii. Idaho (2) Clearwater, Coeur de' Alene
         1. The Palace Entertainment Center
      iii. North Dakota (2) Bismarck, Minot
      iv. Wyoming (3) Cheyenne, Cody, Douglas
   c. The Wagon Wheel Restaurant in Fort Collins

Biography - Vic Swatsek

"After I wrote The Berlin Escape, one of the characters I created named Apollinaris Bonnaire or Apollo for short, seemed to have that unique intrigue and mystery that couldn't fully be explained at the time. I decided to write a separate novel named The Château and expand on her story. Apollo had a sister named Domonique who hadn't spoken to each other in over fifteen years.

This second novel named Retribution was also an offshoot of The Berlin Escape. It takes place primarily in Chile, and Providence, Rhode Island. A powerful individual who will stop at nothing to destroy Walter Donleavy and his empire. He went to great lengths to hide his true identity. He found out too late though, that just having a lot of money was not enough."

Victor Swatsek is the author of **The Prague Deception, The Colorado Conspiracy, The New Mexico Connection, The Amsterdam Protocol, The Moscow Intrigue, The Australian Conclave, The Montana Monopoly, The Italian Illusion, The Berlin Escape, The New York Machinations, and The Château. Retribution** is his twelfth book in the series of his published novels.

All of these books follow several primary characters into thrilling adventures throughout the world. All of his books are written as a series. The first book is *The Prague Deception*, and the latest book is Retribution.

Eight to ten of the same characters are in almost all of his books. The books don't have to be read in that order because each book still stands on its own. However, the first book goes into more detail on the main characters.

"I want to take you on a thrilling journey with action and adventure, romance, mystery, intrigue, and a little history thrown in for good measure. You'll be astounded where my stories will take you."

Victor is a member of the Palm Springs Writers Guild in Southern California, and The Diamond Valley Writers Guild, located in Hemet, California. He has also had several successful book signings.

Victor was born in Austria, and when he was seven years old, the family immigrated to the U.S. He did a tour of duty for the U.S. Army in Virginia, Texas, and Europe, and used this experience in some of his stories.

As the Senior Vice President of Production Operations for a major aerospace company, Vic managed over a thousand employees to produce a product used around the world for the airlines and heavy trucking industry.

He is the first to agree that writing a novel has many additional, interesting, and very challenging facets. His prior business experience has helped him to organize and effectively present very imaginative ideas. He grew up and still lives in Southern California with his wife, Liz.

Many of my FB friends have let me know that they like the fact that my stories are global and not just depicted in one country or city. Those of you that have not gone to my website to see what part of the world all my books will take you, (Recommend using Mozilla Firefox) go to my website, www.NovelsByVic.com "Click" on MAPS, then scroll down to any of my books and it will take you to a flat pattern of the world. There are "pinpoints" which identify the country/state where a part of my story is told.